Ellipsis

Gina Rincavage

Ellipsis
Copyright ©2014 by Gina Rincavage
All rights reserved.

Cover editing and design by Randy Field and Mark Rincavage using James Dylan Photography of model Madelyn Mauch as well as a photograph licensed under Creative Commons Attribution: Author Daniel Majewski.

The artists above do not necessarily endorse this book/author.

The person and events in this book are fictitious. No similarities to actual humans, living or dead, is intended or should be inferred.

ISBN-13: 978-0-692-45782-5
ISBN-10:   0692457828

For my husband, my daughter, my son, and all my family

This story is true…

It's impossible for me to tell the story the way that I remember it…I have to tell the story the way that it really happened. After all, it's not just *my* story…it's Tré's story, it's Aki's story, it's Cameron's story, it's Cohen story…It's *your* story. If it isn't now, it will be…whether you're turning a page, or turning a corner, or bending a knee in a timeless realm…the truth will find you. So if I change narration styles, or include information early that I couldn't have known at the time…please, don't judge me…it's *my story*. Just let me tell it. Because some things aren't going to make sense until the end…

Journey

1 Corinthians 13:12

"Now we see but a poor reflection as in a mirror; then we shall see face to face. Now I know in part; then I shall know fully, even as I am fully known."

Chapter One

On a Miller's Analogy Test that I had to take for grad school, I missed one and only *one* question: FBI is to Shin Bet as CIA is to...Mossad. I guessed Shabak, which is another term for Shin Bet. I guess I was kind of close. Soon I would experientially know the difference. But for now, I was just a girl, sleeping in the most enticing bed in all the world.

His bed. His bed was where I felt at home. It was a warm embrace. A soft caress. An aromatic refuge. Somewhere between being asleep and awake, my only fragment of a coherent thought was that I was where I should be. A fortress. A promise. Similar to the warm embrace of a parent but with the intrigue of a stranger's timely, unforeseen, healing touch.

I open my eyes and take a deep breath in through my nose. The smell warrants further exploration, so I turn into his pillow and inhale with pleasure and intrigue. I turn toward the alarm clock, which beeps dutifully as programmed. I hit it and return to bed. His pillow smells like cologne and a warm fire. His sheets feel like silk, but they are actually a cotton blend and not even a high thread count. The fabric is soft from being worn, and there is nothing else like it on freshly shaven legs. I just love that feeling. I shave every night now. I stretch my legs again and bask in the warmth of his bed. I literally never want to leave it. My hands smooth out the blue sheets in admiration before I grudgingly push myself out of bed. I walk to the closet and open the door. I browse through my somewhat professional clothes and lab coats, which hang next to Tré's jeans and collared shirts. And, I'll be honest, my clothes hanging next to his in the closet must have done something to my brain, because I can't stop thinking about him. And it's not just at the apartment that I think of him. I think about him all the time. His smell is in my clothes and in my hair. His smell lingers on me for hours. When I stand in the genetics lab at New York University, trying to do my thing, analyzing genes, I stop to pull my hair under my nose and think of him. A scientist acting like a foolish schoolgirl.

I unpack my things in his apartment, and I realize that it isn't just pheromones. We have similar interests. I unpack a few videos from a box. I look at them and realize that Tré has the same videos in his entertainment center as I do, one of which is *Casablanca*, one of my all-time favorites. Later I begin to unpack groceries, and I place a bottle of wine in the wine rack next to his wine, with the same label.

But there is one colossal difference between us. He is obviously a Christian, and I *am not*. It's not disdain toward him that you may be sensing. It's disappointment, in that I am sure that *he* wouldn't be truly interested in *me*. I stare up at the replica of the Shroud of Turin that hangs like a shrine above his couch. What interest would he have in a scientist who could quote carbon-14 dates that would shatter his belief system? Although I must say that, as a geneticist, I would love to get my hands on a sample of that DNA, which seems to me to be a little too guarded by popes and those folks at the University of Texas, where it is now stored. I mean, really, if it is that sacred…why not give it a little more exposure?

I move over to view some impressive photographs on the wall and some snapshots of Tré with his friends. He looks like a good person and a nice friend. I really want to know more about him. I glance back over at the Shroud, and realize that, for me, he is the proverbial forbidden fruit. I am thinking about him when the phone rings, which isn't quite a coincidence because I think about him all the time.

"Hello," I answer.

"Journey, hi, how are you? It's Tré."

"Good, how are you?"

"Good. Listen. I just wanted to let you know that my cell phone doesn't work that great here. I go into the city about once a week if you want to leave me a message. If there's an emergency, there's a brochure for the kibbutz near the phone, and they have a landline. They don't always check it, but you can try and leave me a message there if you need to."

"Oh, sure. Thank you," I reply. "How's life on the kibbutz?"

"Great," he responds. "Really nice people and a lot of hard work. I'm sorry I can't talk long; some people are waiting to use this phone."

"Of course."

"Journey…"

"Yes?"

"If my parents call, could you cover for me and tell them to try my cell. I haven't told them I'm here."

"Of course," I reply softly.

"Thanks."

"You're welcome."

"Goodbye."

"Bye."

I guess now is as good a time as any to explain that Tré is not my boyfriend. I hate even the way that that sounds. It sounds like a lie. I love him. But I hardly know him. I am subletting his apartment here in New York. He is a friend of a friend. We met once when he showed me the place and gave me the keys. If anything, I was abrupt with him. I judged him

9

by his looks. I have this thing where if someone is too good-looking, I think they don't know about life. I think they have had it too easy. I think that they are conceited and will surely break my heart. Tré has boyish good looks, light-brown hair, three-day-old scruff, and seafoam-green eyes. Seafoam green. He was super-accommodating and showed me everything from how to turn on the shower to how to make ice. I acted like he was insulting my intelligence. He was going to Israel to work on a kibbutz, and I thought that he was conceited because of his looks. What would life be like for me if people judged me by my looks? Some people say I look like Rachel McAdams. Except, of course, that I have one green eye and one brown eye. I always enjoy the moment when people realize this. It's like they're telling me something I don't know. Sometimes it's taken years for people to notice. And I think it is so strange that some people never do.

···

I am sitting on the couch trying to distract myself from thinking about Tré by reading a textbook when the phone rings.

"Hello?"

"Hello, oh, yes, I'm not sure if I dialed the right number….I'm trying to reach Tré?" A mature female voice is on the line.

"Oh, I'm sorry he's…May I ask who's calling?

"This is his mother."

"Oh, he…left for the weekend, and I'm painting my apartment, and he said that I could stay here," I lie for him.

"I need to get ahold of him," she says, weeping.

"Is everything okay?"

"No, it's his father. His father passed this morning."

"I'm so sorry to hear that. I'll get in touch with him."

"Yes, please. I've left a message on his cell for him to return my call. If you talk to him, would you ask him to call me?"

"Certainly." I hang up the phone and pick up the brochure for the kibbutz.

...

Oh, I tried to call the kibbutz, but the main office was closed for a four day holiday. And before I knew it, I was on a plane to Tel Aviv. My sister, Cindy, is an international flight attendant and free-ticket wizard, so it was no problem for her to get me on a plane.

I stare out the airplane window through the sky. I wasn't there when my father died. I received the news by phone and remember feeling lost. I didn't want that for Tré. Despite the fact that I was doing something crazy for someone I hardly knew, I couldn't help but feel I was doing it for love. It felt a little empowering.

Next I find myself sitting on a bus to Netanya. The brochure had the details of which buses to take to the kibbutz. I thought that the city was beautiful, but I was more taken by the people. They seemed to help one another and were attuned to meet each other's needs. I watch as a religious man helps a mother get her baby's stroller onto the bus, then look over as a well-built young soldier equipped with a rifle steps onto the bus. Despite all the treacherous news about the area, I couldn't help but feel safe. As we travel through the city, I stare out the bus window to see a young man draped in fabric. He has a long beard, appearing almost Christ-like. A young Israeli bus passenger takes notice of my interest and whispers to me in English, "Looks like he's got a case of the Jerusalem syndrome."

"What?" I ask.

"The Jerusalem syndrome—you've never heard of it?"

11

I shake my head, no.

"Some people are completely normal before they come here, but when they arrive in this area, especially Jerusalem, they become a little psychotic, and they think they're a religious figure like Jesus or the Virgin Mary."

I stare at him in disbelief.

"Seriously, it is an actual medical diagnosis."

Soon the bus has stopped at my destination. I walk up the path to the kibbutz. I have no idea how I will tell Tré the bad news.

One thing that I distinctly remember from my father's death was that no one seemed to say the right thing. Actually, an older gentleman in the biology department had said that he was sorry and that he had "been there," and it brought great comfort to me.

The dirt path leads straight into the vineyard. I stop walking because I am breathless at the sight of Tré standing in the vineyard with a basket in his hands. As he works, he smiles while talking with a friend. He looks up at me, and I feel paralyzed. He places his basket on the ground and walks toward me and then begins to lightly jog up to me. His smile fades as he sees the seriousness on my face. I don't want to do this.

"What are you doing here?" he asks.

"I'm bringing you some news that's...not good."

"What? What is it?"

I can't hold back the tears. "Your father..."

He gives me a remorseful, yet comforting hug. He doesn't make me say it, and that's good because I don't quite know how. He puts his arm around me and leads me toward the dormitories.

"I'm sorry, I don't have any details. I was so shocked when your mother called. I didn't tell her you were here. I have a ticket reserved for you to Newark, and then on to Fort Worth." Tré hugs my waist a little tighter.

...

We sat together on the bus and on the plane but didn't say much. I held his hand and felt a little ashamed to think that it felt very good. His hands were calloused, like a man's should be.

When we arrive in Newark, I open a locker and present him with his suitcase. "I hope you don't mind. I packed your bag for you. You just had one black suit in the closet. I thought that you would want to get there as soon as you could."

"Thank you...you've been so wonderful."

"Do you want to check and see if there is anything else you need? There are shoes, socks...everything." I didn't know if I should say "boxers."

"I don't know if I could actually get my thoughts together enough to pack. Thank you, really, you've been an angel."

I waited with him until his plane left. He hugged me goodbye and held on to me like he didn't want to let go. I know that I didn't imagine that. But I couldn't help noticing that there was an emptiness in his eyes. And when I look back it's evident that he had lost more than his father that day.

...

A few days later, I hear a knock at the door. I open it to find Tré, with his luggage in his hand. I stifle my shock and excitement and open the door wider to welcome him in. His eyes are a little red and slightly swollen. He looks as if he has lost a few pounds in those few days. He smells just as I remembered, ambrosial. I can feel my heart pound and my hands shake at just the sight of him, but I try to calm the excitement in my voice.

"Hi," I say. "I would've picked you up from the airport."

13

"Please, this is New York. I'm no stranger to the cab ride."

When I hug him, I notice he is a little slow to hug back.

"How are you?" I ask.

He gets one tear in his eye that refuses to come out. "It was really hard for me...all of this. All I wanted to do was get back here, to this apartment. I wanted to be there for my family, but I was really having a hard time with my grief *and* theirs. It was like everything I was feeling, I was imagining that they were feeling, too, and I think that was a little too much for me."

"Of course." I try to comfort him. I hug him again. Would you like something to drink?" I offer.

"That would be great," Tré says thankfully.

"Water or wine?"

"Wine, please."

"Are you hungry? I was just about to make dinner. Would you like to join me, or do you need to lie down?" I ask.

"I feel at home here. I'll join you, of course. Thank you."

In the kitchen, Tré slices onions like a chef. I stand by his side and slice mushrooms. His cologne radiates through the room, and I think of how immensely grateful I feel to be cooking with him. I ignore the fact that just the act of making dinner with him is orchestrating my brain chemistry into stabilizing the thought that we might one day be together.

"I have to say that you turned me onto this jasmine rice," I say.

"It is good."

"And this is the second bottle of this soy sauce that I've bought."

"From the oriental store around the corner?"

14

"I wish I could have called you, I looked everywhere for it. Then to find it around the corner."

We grow silent for a moment.

"It was really nice what you did. I mean, not being able to call me and traveling to Israel," he says.

"I was happy to...That came out wrong...I have a passport and was glad that I was able to."

"So what other things have you stolen from me?" Tré lightens the mood.

"Are you talking about me *borrowing* your soy sauce? I replaced it, remember? I also borrowed your John Mayer CD."

"Keep it," he says, looking a little embarrassed.

"What? You don't like him?"

"I like him. I just didn't want anyone to know I had that CD."

We continue with our small talk as we cook. We are using my recipe, but he has added spice to it, and it turns out better than anything I have ever made. I am starting to think he is naturally good at everything.

"So basically there is no mystery to me. You've slept in my bed, you've packed my underwear, and you've practically seen me cry," he says as we finish the meal. With each bite that he took I had to force myself not to stare at his angular jawline and the way his jaw muscle flexed with each bite.

"Yeah, your underwear, I wasn't too sure about that." I try to stay focused on the conversation.

"No. Thank you. If you had left those out, I would have been very uncomfortable. I probably would've made some other people feel uncomfortable too." He smiles with his perfectly straight teeth that are whiter than mine. His cuspids are long and very pointed. Okay, so there are certain little things that I like and look for in a man. Calloused hands and

15

pointy cuspid teeth are on the list. They are not a requirement. I am *not* superficial; I just like anything that looks predominantly male, like Adam's apples and facial hair. It's genetic predisposition. It's natural selection. We choose our mates based on signs of virility, to insure the continuation of our species. It's a survival instinct, really.

With him, I could have talked superficially all night and been happy just looking at him. But would he ultimately be able to keep my attention? I have to know. I search to find a way to segue into the deep. I come up empty but try to start somewhere.

"I love your artwork," I say, referring to the array of artistic photographs that he has displayed throughout his home.

"Thank you."

The humility in his "thank you" sparks an interest in me. "Who is the artist?" I ask. "I noticed they aren't signed."

"I took them," he replies, equally as humble.

"They're amazing. You are a true artist," I say impressed.

"I…I just *take* the pictures."

"Do you sell them?"

"I finance my trips through them. Do you have a favorite?" he asks.

My first thought goes to the Shroud of Turin, which is obviously a print, not his. I adamantly ignore it, not believing it to be true. I desperately try to put it out of my mind. "They are all wonderful, really. But I guess the one of Israel stands out."

He smiles. "They are almost all, of Israel."

I feel embarrassed now, like I haven't *really* seen them.

"You mean the one of the Wailing Wall," he presumes, correctly.

"Yes."

"I want you to have it."

"Wow! Thank you," I say. "Will you sign it?"

"I really don't like to put my signature on them. It just doesn't feel right to me." *He* took the conversation deeper all on his own.

"Why Israel?" I continue to test the water. Exactly how deep is he?

"Israel? I think of it as, when you really love someone, or at least when you are infatuated with someone—you would appreciate anyone who could help bring you and that person together. I wanted to be that person for God. I wanted to help bridge the gap." He is deep.

"Are you going back?"

"I feel a little lost, so I think it's better that I do. I was wondering if I could stay on a day or two, to ground myself." He seems to be thinking this through for the first time.

"You're welcome to stay here; this is your apartment. I could get a hotel if it helps you," I say politely. I am *so* not getting a hotel.

"If you don't mind staying, I could sleep on the couch."

Now we're talking. Breathe—I remind myself. "Under the shrine?" I ask tauntingly.

Tré smiles, then looks over at the replica of the Shroud of Turin.

"That's not sacrilegious?" I continue.

"You recognize the image? It's the negative image replica of the Shroud of Turin."

We both walk over to stand in front of it, as if we are discussing an item on display at a museum.

"I know what it is. An ancient burial cloth. Some believe that it belonged to Jesus Christ." I need him to know… I'm intelligent. Why is this so important to me? Because I can tell that *he is* intelligent.

"You say 'some' so condescendingly," Tré says, surprisingly amused.

"Well, maybe you've heard of a little something called carbon-14 dating, which refuted this theory," I counter.

"Carbon-14 dating: measuring the half-life of the radioactive isotope carbon-14 to determine the age of organic material. I suppose that you didn't hear that the fungi found on the cloth skewed those results," he asserts back with a smile.

I bite my lip and try not to argue. I am getting mad. He is enjoying the intellectual conversation, and I am getting mad. How juvenile of me. I start to forget myself altogether as I look at him. He looks deeply and lovingly at the replica.

"You don't believe in God at all?" he asks, full of concern for me.

"I'm a scientist."

"If science is so great, why has it yet to explain what caused this image to appear on the cloth? Just look at it…the crown of thorns, the pierced hands and feet, linear wounds on the torso and legs consistent with beatings, and no evidence of fractured bones."

"I know the theories…I've seen the shroud in person, in Italy, as a child," I say.

Tré turns to me and stares deeply into my eyes. Seafoam green. "What was it like to see the shroud in person?" he asks.

"It was captivating. Here I was, this six-year-old girl, staring at the cloth I was told was sacred. I stood there refusing to leave. I think my parents were actually embarrassed."

"How did you *feel*?" Tré looks very invested in my response.

"I felt like my soul was too big for my body. And then I fainted."

"You fainted?"

"Yeah. Well, you have to understand that this is nothing unusual for me. I faint whenever I stand for too long. As a child I explained this phenomenon as 'brown carpet and yellow flowers.' When I would start to lose my field of vision, I described it as seeing brown carpet. And when the yellow flowers appeared on the carpet, I knew I was going down and there wasn't anything I could do about it. I fainted at virtually every Christmas program I participated in, in school. The fainting and the *feeling* were two separate sensations that happened to occur together when I saw the shroud."

"So the *feeling*…Do you still get that?"

I couldn't believe it. As he asked that, the *feeling* rushed over me like a wave. I hadn't felt it since that day, as a child. And yet, in this moment, it was so powerful and unexplainable. It overwhelmed my heart, my mind, and my emotions with a pleasurable essence of warmth, safety, and love. The *feeling* seemed strangely more than physical. The second it left, I longed for more.

"No," I lied. Why? I don't know. Maybe I was just a little scared.

"I get that feeling pretty often. It's good." He smiles.

I thought he was lying too.

"It's His Spirit testifying to your spirit that this is the truth," he explains nonchalantly. He touches my chest as he explains about the Spirit.

I feel the wave come over me again, and I invite it in. I try desperately to hold onto it a little longer.

I realize his hand is still resting on my chest. I take a deep breath in. The smell of his cologne fills my nostrils. What started as an innocent gesture puts us face to face in a rather intimate position. I reach up to grasp his hand. He touches my face with his other hand. We start to kiss, passionately. He carries me in the kiss to his bedroom, and away from the replica of the shroud.

We continue kissing on his bed. At one point he stops and just looks at me. It's as if, through this gesture, he is offering a way out, a moment for me to think and regain composure. This look offers possible freedom from what he believes is a sinful act. Neither of us takes the way out. I pull him closer and with this consensual agreement, he begins to undress me.

...

In the morning, when I open my eyes, I find myself in Tré's embrace. He caresses me and gives me a kiss on the cheek.

"I'm a sorry excuse for a Christian," he says.

"Don't say that."

"Please forgive me." He is still caressing me and almost desperately holding on to me.

"Why? Have you made a mistake?" I ask, hiding my hurt.

"I can only confuse you."

"I'm not sorry. And I'm not going to apologize for how I feel," I insist.

He swallows hard.

He made me the best omelet I had ever had. And although he was genuinely affectionate with me, I knew he was leaving and that he might never be back. And as far as I was concerned, he was taking God with him. This made me sad, and at the time I didn't realize that I would later lose sleep about the thought of letting not one but *both* of them go forever.

The cab that will take him away honks, and Tré gives me a hug and a kiss. The kiss takes a passionate turn. The cab driver honks again and Tré gently breaks away from me.

"I have to go," he says apologetically.

I don't say anything. There is no point in debating. I know that he is going back to Israel, his first love. *He* is mine. I had thought that science was my first love, but there is *no comparison*. I have tasted the fruit, and I know that it is good.

And just like that, he was gone.

Chapter Two

We kept in touch, but he was distant. I didn't want to push him. The outcome of our relationship was his choice. I tried to fight the fact that I was still interested in him and, quite possibly, God. I looked into the Jerusalem syndrome and found that Kfar Shaul Hospital, in Jerusalem, was offering a fellowship for geneticists. I applied for it. You know I did. But I applied for the fellowship at Johns Hopkins, too. From the time I knew what a DNA strand was, I had wanted to be there.

I was shocked to receive the reply letter from Johns Hopkins so quickly. I wasn't sure if that was a good sign or not. I wasn't sure that going there was really what I wanted anymore. Or did I want to be in Israel with Tré? Would it be too much of a sacrifice, to let my career follow an unscheduled route? Or would taking a chance in moving to Israel reorder the life I had mapped out since I was a child? The truth is, I felt more alive when I was around Tré. I felt like I understood more about myself around him. But again, I could move to Israel and still face the fact that Tré was not interested in a relationship with me. I could easily torture myself with the many scenarios. I hold the letter close to my chest. I touch the return address in disbelief. I rub my fingers over the glued seal on the back of the envelope, but I stop short of opening it. I place it on the bar and back away from it as if it might actually explode. I sit on the couch and stare at it for a long while. Then, I fumble through my purse for my cell phone and walk over to my laptop and look up the number for Kfar Shaul Hospital. I dial.

A young man answers in Hebrew, and I feel a little rude about ignoring his Hebrew as I proceed to speak English. From my trip over there I am aware that practically everyone, especially everyone under the age of fifty, speaks English.

"Could I have Dr. Oberstein's floor please?"

They transfer the phone call, and I again ignore the Hebrew and proceed in English, "Yes, is Dr. Oberstein available?"

Another young man answers, "This is Yonathan, Dr. Oberstein's assistant. He is with a patient. Is there something that I can help you with?"

"Yes, my name is Journey Kaufmann. I applied for the fellowship in genetics."

"Ah, yes, Journey Kaufmann. You're calling about an interview?"

"What?"

"Oh, that's right. I hadn't called you yet. You have been selected to be interviewed for the position. How does the fourteenth at two o'clock sound?"

"Are you talking about a telephone interview?" I try to clarify.

"Dr. Oberstein doesn't do telephone interviews," Yonathan replies, as if my question were utterly ridiculous.

"That sounds great," I somehow manage to say. "I'll be there."

I hang up the phone and am keenly aware that I'm sitting on the couch beneath the replica of the Shroud of Turin. I have ignored the artifact since the day that Tré and I reviewed it together. I have ignored it but have not forgotten it. Part of me takes comfort in the fact that it is there. Part of me is very intrigued by its timely reappearance in my life. I imagine that, if there is a God who wants to know me, if He is interested in me, I would have to be interested in Him as well.

After all, I am a good person. I care deeply about people. I have devoted my life to helping others. But my devotion is also to science and what it offers. I like things that can be explained. I have always excelled in math. I enjoy the idea that something can be either right or wrong, and that there is no objective surveyor that can misinterpret my intent. It is also very important to me that my integrity exists when no one is looking. My opinion of myself matters far more than the opinion that others have of me, although that is held in my utmost regard as well. For example, I notice that Tré has a stack of family albums in his closet that I would thoroughly enjoy looking at. Just to know him better. And although I feel confident that he wouldn't mind if I were to view them, I refuse to even take a peek. This has to be off limits. His privacy is important. It would be nice to have that insight though. And his medicine cabinet is a closed patient chart to me. I will not dare to venture into. I can be very legalistic. This has to mean something to God…if He exists…right?

...

The very next day, I receive a call from Dr. Rosenbaum, my professor and mentor in genetics. He tells me that he has received a call from Dr. Oberstein.

"He seemed very interested in hiring you," Dr. Rosenbaum says.

"What do you think?" I ask.

"I've known Dr. Oberstein for years. He's a genius, really. I think it would be a smart move for you…an interesting move. Journey, you'd be in good hands." His voice softens. "The premise for his research is to establish whether or not the Jerusalem syndrome is an illness that occurs in the general population or more predominantly in those who have a genetic predisposition for psychosis. The research will be statistically significant either way. This means publication for you. When you get that publication, you know that our faculty will hire you if you ever want to join us. I admitted to him that we wanted you back, if you were ever willing."

"Wow. Thank you. I'm honored," I say. "Did you really mean that?"

"Of course. Journey, he's a brilliant psychiatrist. You can't lie to *that man,* and you know I would never lie to you."

"What about Johns Hopkins?"

"What about Johns Hopkins? I think you will find that Israeli technology is pretty remarkable. I think you should carefully weigh your options, but personally, I think moving to Israel might be a smarter move."

"Thank you," I say again, which he takes as a goodbye.

"You're welcome and best of luck to you, Journey." He hangs up.

Why do physicians have this thing where they are always giving report and never saying goodbye? And I am one of them. I put my phone down and think about his conversation. His input is persuasive. I appreciate that Dr. Rosenbaum had my back. *Dr. Rosenbaum.* It dawns on me that his input is probably culturally biased. I consider him a mentor and a friend, but I *will* carefully weigh my options. I have a Jewish name also, but my family has long since departed from its roots, tradition, and religion.

•••

And with another wave of my sister's magical international flight wand, I arrive safely in Israel again.

Tel Aviv. Cab ride. Jerusalem hotel. I sleep relatively well after being up all night on the redeye. The next day when

I wake up, I shower and dress for the interview. I choose to take a bus to Kfar Shaul Hospital. I want to experience what it is like to be a local.

As I near the hospital, I can see a man walking down the street wearing nothing but a hospital gown and his underwear, which is revealed by the gown's open back. He is talking to his hand. People on the bus are pointing and whispering. I think I hear them say "Jerusalem syndrome" and take it as my cue. I get off at the next stop. I have to walk quickly toward him, which is away from the hospital, just to catch up. I am a little out of breath by the time I reach him.

"Excuse me," I say several times before he turns his head and the fingers of his hand towards me.

"Who are you talking to?" he asks in a thick English accent.

"You…of course," I say looking at him, and *not* his hand.

"Yes?" he asks politely. His fingers are still pointed toward me as if they are listening, as well.

"Well, I am having this problem. I have to get to Kfar Shaul Hospital and I am having trouble finding it. I saw you and thought that you might be so kind as to help me," I say, taking care to be equally polite.

"It's just up the street there, on the right," he says as he continues to walk away from the hospital. He has clearly discharged himself against medical advice and in a hurry.

"I'm not very good with directions and uh…" I bite my lip for effect as I continue, "I really need to get there." I say this in a desperate tone, trying to suggest that I am visiting someone.

"You poor girl. Well *he* is desperately looking for his staff," he says nodding toward his hand. "And I would do just about anything for a cup of *Earl Grey* right now, or I would help you."

"Moses?" I ask, as I peripherally view a coffee shop.

"Yes," he says excitedly.

"I would love to buy you a cup of tea."

He feels for his absent back pocket and wallet and realizes that this is a gracious offer. He follows me into the coffee shop, and I can feel every eye on us. The young worker quickly obliges my request in English, giving me a knowing look. I consider the barista's look an invitation to seek support from him. "I was just telling Moses that I really need to get to Kfar Shaul Hospital, and I was hoping that he could help me," I say.

"I told her that it was just up the street. She can't miss it," Moses says.

The Israeli doesn't miss a beat. "It would be nice if you could take her there yourself. After all she did treat you." He hands us two to-go cups, my coffee and his tea.

"I can't drink tea out of paper," Moses says snobbishly.

The coffee shop worker pours another serving into a real teacup. "You can take it with you," he says generously. "Cream?" he asks.

"Milk and honey please," Moses replies.

"You'll help the girl?" The worker asks before adding his condiments, as if it were conditional.

"Yes, I'd be glad to," Moses says, completely accepting the bribe.

"Milk and honey," the worker says as he adds them. "Of course."

He hands him the tea. Moses' hand takes a break from its stiff attentiveness and accepts the cup of tea as a fair trade for the missing staff, for now.

A female Israeli soldier approaches the counter as we turn from it.

"A to-go cup?" The worker asks presumptuously, in English for my benefit.

"Yes," she says and winks at me.

She follows us, at a safe distance, to the hospital. Moses is oblivious of anything but his well-earned tea. The whole chain of events seems nothing short of miraculous, considering my "business" in Israel, as the customs official worded it. I feel a camaraderie with Israelis through this, and I'll be the first one to say that *I* am impressed by *them*.

...

Yonathan, Dr. Oberstein's assistant, greets me, along with my trophy AMA patient, at Kfar Shaul Hospital. I introduce myself to him and let him know that the *nice man* helped me find the place. Nurses gather around Moses and usher him towards the dayroom.

Yonathan looks to be in his twenties, with square, black-framed glasses that rest on his prominent nose. He squints his cheeks to push them up instead of using his finger. Resourceful. "Impressive," he says, referring to my patient retrieval tactics. He ushers me down the hallway towards Dr. Oberstein's office. "You look like a young Rachel McAdams," he says conversationally.

"I get that a lot," I say politely but ponder the "young" reference. I feel the need to affirm that he has gotten my résumé, to be sure that he knows I am old enough to have made it through medical school. How old is Rachel McAdams anyway? And why am I so insecure about this job…because I *want* it. "You did get my résumé, right?" I ask.

"Your résumé has been thoroughly reviewed or you wouldn't be here. Dr. Oberstein doesn't believe in wasting time," he says, as if I had insulted them both. We reach Dr. Oberstein's door and enter with permission.

"Journey brought Mr. Abrams back," Yonathan informs Dr. Oberstein, apparently referring to Moses. Yonathan takes a seat in the armchair next to Dr. Oberstein's desk to stay for the interview.

"Thank you," Dr. Oberstein says with a smile. He stands up and comes around his desk to shake my hand and introduce himself. "Please have a seat," he says gesturing to the chair right in front of his desk. He returns to his seat.

I find myself staring Dr. Oberstein squarely in the eyes as he peers over my paperwork with his round, wire-rimmed spectacles. His glossy bald head shines under the overhead fluorescent lighting. His full, white, meticulously trimmed beard suggests to me that he is a man who is concerned with details and thoroughness. He has the look and mannerisms of Zola Levitt, not someone I followed, just someone I was aware of.

"Well, I would ask how you became interested in genetics, but I think that is evident by just looking at you," Dr. Oberstein says and I can only assume he is referring to my oddly paired eye color. He is observant.

"Nicely deduced," I say.

"You have a very intellectual résumé," he says, but seems to be disappointed somehow. It's as if my high credentials had left him with no other option, but he is still unsure about choosing me. Something is wrong. I can't figure out what it is. He doesn't want *me* for some reason.

"Thank you," I respond.

"Is all of this true?" Dr. Oberstein inquires, narrowing the circumference of his eyes.

"Of course," I respond coolly. "My mentor, Dr. Rosenbaum, informed me that he received a call from you. I was pleasantly surprised to learn that you are friends." I let him know I know what he knows. So why the questioning?

He softens, "He had the kindest things to say about you. And yes, he validated your application submission. You are a good researcher…How are you with people?"

"I enjoy working with people." How original. There is a moment of silence, and I am painfully unable to concentrate on anything other than the low hum of the fluorescent lights above.

"You understand that your job here would be to persuade crazy people to give you their blood. We do it here. You will be doing it on the streets. You will, of course, try to get the patients to the hospital," Dr. Oberstein says.

Yonathan chimes in, "Here at the hospital we establish a clinical relationship with our patients. We take time to build rapport and establish trust. On the streets you have to be able to do that in a millisecond. This is a very social position. It would be a good job for…a homecoming queen."

Without hesitation I say, "I was the homecoming queen." This is true.

"Are there any other fellowship offers you're considering?" Dr. Oberstein asks almost accusingly.

I realize he needs to know that I have other options. I *want* him to know I have other options. I want him to know that I am choosing him and not just the other way around. "I think Johns Hopkins would take me."

"Johns Hopkins? What makes you think that?" Dr. Oberstein reveals a generous smile. He lets go of the paperwork in his hands. Oh, now I have his attention. I take the letter from Johns Hopkins, still unopened, out of my purse and hand it to him.

"You haven't opened it," he tests me.

Yes, this is a gamble, but I am all in now. "I was waiting to see if you would take me," I say with unexplainable confidence.

"It's an awfully light letter," he says pointing out the obvious and suggesting it is not the typical parcel size for an acceptance packet.

"Would you like to open it?" I ask, almost too cocky, so I shrug my shoulders and try my best to now look innocent.

"It's addressed to you," he counters. Okay, so is this Jewish legalism at its best? Is he toying with me?

"Bevakasha." I invite him to open it with one of the only Hebrew words that I know. Dr. Oberstein places the envelope on his desk. Yonathan stares at it.

Yonathan takes the reins, "Allow me?"

I nod. Yonathan opens the letter. He looks at it ever so briefly and then hands it into Dr. Oberstein's open and waiting hands. Dr. Oberstein looks slightly impressed. I try to look uninterested.

"This is a dangerous job. Why should I hire a woman?" Dr. Oberstein asks. Now we are getting somewhere. This is the problem. He envisioned hiring a man.

I am wearing a short-sleeved business shirt. I did forgo the suit after all; this is Israel. I scratch a nonexistent itch on my bicep just to flex it. His eyes follow me there. He is thoroughly assessing me. A good physician. "I'm a sixth-degree black belt in karate," I reply. This is true.

"You'll need to learn Israeli martial arts," Dr. Oberstein challenges.

"Krav Maga. Already an interest," I assure him. True.

"Any questions for me?" Dr. Oberstein asks.

"When should I expect to hear back?" I ask.

"Tomorrow morning," Dr. Oberstein assures me. He's a man who is not afraid to make a decision.

I tear off a piece of the Johns Hopkins letter to use as scrap paper. I write my hotel name and number on the back of the letter and hand it to Dr. Oberstein.

"Here's my hotel name and number...you have my cell."

Dr. Oberstein looks slightly amused as he accepts it. He looks over at Yonathan, "Would you be so kind as to give Dr. Kaufmann a tour of our lab and the hospital?"

"Certainly," Yonathan responds and starts to escort me out, but not before Dr. Oberstein gives me a handshake, warmly adding his other hand for a brief moment. His smile genuine, his professionalism intact, and a glimmer of promise in his eyes.

The lab and hospital are more than impressive. I don't know what I was expecting or if I even cared, but it is obvious that no expense has been spared concerning their technology. They value the science and art of genetics.

Chapter Three

I was nervous about calling Tré but managed to arrange for us to have lunch. We decided to meet on Ben Yehuda Street.

The brick-lined street has an array of shops and cafés. The locals seem to swarm in and out of the stores. There are people laughing and talking. I see people engaged in what looks like a heated argument, and then, all of a sudden, one of them will laugh and then they appear to be the best of friends. The smell of Mediterranean food fills the air. I pass several musicians playing for those strolling by. The musicians seem young and truly talented. There is a nervous ache in my stomach and my hands begin to shake. I know Tré is close, and it literally makes me weak. I can see that he is seated at the outdoor café where we have arranged to meet, and I try not to look lost. He stands and greets me with an Israeli kiss on the cheek. I sit down to join him.

"It was nice of you to meet me here. It was a lot easier to phone you at your new kibbutz," I say.

"What brings you here?" he asks, looking excited to see me.

"I flew here for an interview at Kfar Shaul Hospital."

"How did it go?"

"We'll see…How are you?"

"Good. Working. Getting a farmer's tan." He lifts up his sleeve to display it. I smile at him and again admire his snow-white teeth.

"How are you really?" My question seems to penetrate through his superficial pleasantries.

Tré is silent. He shifts in his chair. He swallows hard. One eye seems to have slightly more lubrication than necessary. He sees my penetrating question and ups the ante with his philosophical one, "When my father died, did everything I believe die with him?"

"Can faith die?" I tread in the theological water that I am so unfamiliar with. My question is searching and yet accusatory at the same time. I desperately want what he has to be real, spiritually.

Tré is astonished by my response. "This, from someone who doesn't believe?" he asks, baffled.

I want to tell him that I felt what he called "God's Spirit" the last day we were together, but I don't. "I believe in your faith. I just don't have any personally...," I say.

"Yet," Tré adds. He reaches for my hand. He interlaces his fingers with mine. He opens his hand and holds his palm and fingers against mine, as if he wished he could actually transfer what little faith he has left over to me. And then he lets go as if somehow he seemed to remember that because of my faithlessness, I am off limits.

"You should know that I just really want to try to get my relationship right with God before I add anyone else to it." His honesty may be a bit too hard for me to swallow.

"And when you do get it right, could a good Christian be with someone who doesn't believe?" I test his honesty further. Not to make light of his pain or his spiritual toil, I feel like I need to know where I stand. I feel that, despite his grief, he owes me that.

"Honestly...No. It's probably better if we don't see each other. I can't be someone that I am not, and I don't want to hurt you any more than I already have." The boy is honest, if anything. I've got to give him that.

The waitress comes to take our order, which seems kind of irrelevant now. "I think we've had a change of heart," I tell her. I stand up to leave, as does Tré. There's nothing worse than trying to eat when you feel like crying. We start to walk away together, and I turn to him and say, "I still want to be there for you, as a friend."

"I don't think that's possible for me." He embraces me and kisses me with an ever-so-brief but intense kiss.

The way he kissed me, I knew he meant what he said. This felt like goodbye. Then we walked away from each other. I believe in not looking back in the very literal sense of it.

The next morning, I sit on the balcony of my hotel room and admire the Old City. It is truly majestic with its golden dome, walled with ancient walls, both of which declare the division of two faiths on one ceremonially sacred ground. A rival between brothers: one chosen, the other despised. Both insisting they are called of God…His chosen son. I am merely a spectator of their beliefs, coveting them both, hoping that it is possible to believe beyond myself, feeling especially despised myself, for not having a belief to call my own, refusing to believe that I, too, could be chosen of God.

The phone rings. It is Dr. Oberstein. He has called to say I am the first and only choice for the fellowship.

I accept eagerly. "When can I start?"

"Let me ask you that. When can you start?"

"To be honest, I came here on a one way ticket. I can start anytime."

"Get over your jet lag, find a place to stay. Consider the Abu Tor neighborhood, it's fairly near the Old City. It's a mixed Jewish and Arab neighborhood, and the apartments are often easy to rent. Get to know the city, visit the Western

Wall and come into the hospital in a few days to a week. You are on the clock."

"Is this doctor's orders?"

"Always."

"Thank you."

...

The cab ride through the Abu Tor neighborhood confirms Dr. Oberstein's description. Jewish boys wearing their kippot casually walk past Arab women wearing hijab. The two drastically different people of faith, living side by side in apparently perfect peace. I sit in a cab with a mature English realtor who has reiterated what Dr. Oberstein had said about this desirable neighborhood.

"You missed it by one street," the realtor says to the cab driver. The street we are on now begins the downslope overlooking the valley per se. The architecture appears older and smaller. An Arab girl not more than four or five throws a rock at the cab. I am appalled, as if I have witnessed a rare occurrence of such a social faux pas. The realtor tries to alleviate my disillusionment. "I'm sorry…that happens. They learn it. But for the most part, you can see, Arabs and Jews live next to each other with no reservation. They are neighbors, and this is their way of life. And most Muslims are faithful, kind people."

The cab stops on the correct street in front of a modern-looking complex. The realtor walks up the stairs on the leftmost unit which is set above a basement unit. She opens the door for me. The place is relatively spacious, with balconies off the living room area and upstairs bedroom. The large stone floors are a pinkish tone and reflect light. Settling cracks can be seen down most of the walls, but that only seems natural.

"I cleaned the entire place this morning. See how the floor shines. We do get a lot of dust," she says.

"I don't feel like I need to see another place."

"I don't think you do either, dear. The neighbor to your left is an older lady. She is kind of like the neighborhood watch. In the standalone relic beside you, there is also a fifty-something, newly widowed lady who is off on an archeological dig. She seems to have a very nice gentleman subletting the place. That should make you feel safe."

The realtor opens the balcony doors off the living room. I have to take in a breath with the view. The air is arid and dusty. The once-monotonous off-white drab of the housing and stone buildings appears harmoniously beautiful when overlooking them. I take another deep breath in through my nostrils, to enjoy the fragrant smells of heavily spiced Arab food. Children's laughter can be heard from even far away. The line-hung, colorful laundry that decorates most of the balconies is homage to a simpler way of life, I have yet to learn.

"I'll take it," I say.

···

Moving in was just a matter of bringing my suitcase over. I had learned to live like this since I decided to follow the winding roads of my educational career.

I sit on the balcony and again absorb the view of the sea of white architecture that *is* Jerusalem. In my hand I have a glass of Mount Carmel wine, a gift from the "dear" realtor. I take a sip of this amazing wine and look at it in disbelief, undoubtedly the best wine I have ever tasted. I am so intoxicated by the view that I don't notice that my male neighbor has also exited onto his back balcony. I vaguely notice that he seems to look over at me a few times, but I am too engrossed in the view and the thoughts of my day to even give him the time of day.

The next day, being the good little employee that I am, I follow my instructions and take the short walk to the Old City to visit the Wailing Wall. I stand in line for the security check. The line is moving very slowly. I can see a group of young Jewish teenagers sitting in a circle singing what can only be Hebrew praise songs. There is something so right and beautiful about the act of the young singing to God that I feel moved. I only wish that I could share this moment with someone that I know. I stare at the Wailing Wall and the mostly religious Jews in their dutiful black, bowing that perpetual bow, and I am amazed that a people could wait endlessly on their seemingly absent Messiah. This, to me, is almost incomprehensible and yet very...endearing. I stand in awe of them, perhaps a little too long, because I start to see brown carpet...and yellow flowers. Pulsating yellow flowers start to appear on the brown like the shapes in a kaleidoscope. Then the flowers lose their shape and the brown dissipates as the blue of the sky appears, with its soft clouds. And then I see a face, a man's face.

"I'm okay." Although my hearing is just now returning, I assume from experience that I have been asked about my condition.

"I'm okay," I repeat, a little more assertively.

His face is warm and attentive. He is attractive, but my pride makes my concern about regaining my composure.

He smiles at me and says assuredly, "You're okay."

I realize that I am in his arms, and I politely struggle to stand. Face-to-face with him, his eyes for the first time give meaning to the term "deep pools"...concentric circles to infinity...I could easily fall into...drown in....His are brown. I am mesmerized. I almost lose track of my thoughts. I notice that people have begun to stare at me, and I announce, "It's just a thing, when I stand too long. It happens. Really, I'm fine." I take a closer look at him. I feel like I know him from somewhere. "Your face looks familiar, have I seen you before?"

"I'm your neighbor, Cohen."

"Oh, yes. I'm sorry I haven't been more neighborly, I really just moved in," I say grasping at words to appear normal.

"I would've come over and introduced myself, but you were just looking pretty absorbed on the balcony," he says with a smile.

"Well it's a nice view," I say, feeling much better.

The line for the men and women starts to divide. It seems a little sexist that they can't worship together, but I am willing to learn.

"Come by anytime, Journey," Cohen says as our lines separate.

I follow the other women towards the Wall. I look in my purse for some paper, feeling a little unprepared. I tear another piece off of my Johns Hopkins letter and write a prayer. I fold the piece of paper and stand before the Wall. The Wall is so worn from the touch of prayerful hands that it feels like polished soapstone. I feel unworthy to stand there, where more honest people have been. I wedge my prayer into the Wall. I look to the others for direction and start to back away from the Wall reverently. Then a strong, ambient male voice begins to sing the Shema, reverently, passionately, unexplainably amplified. Everyone looks and sees it is coming from an almost unlikely source. A man with very short hair, dressed in jeans and a leather jacket, is standing in the center of the Wall between the male and female sides with his back to the Wall. People seem to be frozen in time. And it

39

is a complete mystery whether it is the vibration of his voice or if the Wall actually shook, but hundreds and hundreds of prayers that have been wedged in the Wall come loose, are caught in an unseasonable wind, and come down like confetti at a Mardi Gras parade. Just then Cohen pats a man—much later I will learn that his name is Aki—on the back and attempts to hand him one of the folded prayers. When Aki turns to Cohen, it is evident that he is an attractive Israeli man standing at a distance from the Wall.

"Is this yours?" Cohen asks in Hebrew. I have no idea what they are saying, it is just one facet of an unworldly event.

Aki points to all the flying pieces of paper. "Look!" he replies in Hebrew. "They're everywhere. Don't you see what the man is doing?" He is annoyed but accepts the paper from Cohen anyway and begins to run toward the man who is singing loudly. Israeli security have already closed in on the man that Aki is pursuing, but they have yet to apprehend him. They seem not quite sure what to do. As Aki approaches the singer, he takes out a badge with a picture ID.

"Arrest this man," Aki orders the security men in Hebrew.

The security forces turn their focus from the singer, who is singing the last phrase of the song, seemingly unthreatened by their approach, to Aki.

One of the security men now addresses Aki in Hebrew, and with commanding authority, "Sir, where did you get that badge?"

Aki appears baffled by the insubordination and continues in Hebrew, even more annoyed, "Arrest him!"

When Aki makes a move toward the singer himself, Israeli security take Aki by both arms and begin to escort him to their post.

Israeli security continue to question Aki in their national language, "Sir, where did you get that badge?" The only thing I am cognizant of between them is that the security men have apprehended Aki, the plainclothesman. They are clearly more interested in him than the singer.

For me, the singer is much more intriguing. He walks quickly away and I, along with others, follow him. As I follow the singer, I can see a beautiful Israeli woman approach Cohen. Very soon I will meet her and learn that her name is Cameron. She puts her hand in Cohen's and stares deeply into his eyes. The fallen prayers still circling. The frozen visitors have moved into panic mode and move chaotically out of the area. Cameron and Cohen move closer to each other. She hesitantly touches his face. He lets her move into an embrace, and it actually looks as though two lost lovers are reuniting. He holds her adoringly as the crowd seems to move in fast forward around them. The two seem to be engrossed only in each other.

I follow the singer as he moves quickly through the Christian quarter. A woman who is following him with me asks him, "Who are you?"

He only smiles and continues on. We follow him down the street. A reporter, with her cameraman, walks right past us.

She asks her colleague in Hebrew, "What happened? Was there a small quake?"

As the singer walks out of the area, a baker hands him several loaves of challah bread and a large bottle of water. The baker then says, "Shabbat shalom, Melchizedek, for you and your friends." The followers help Melchizedek, the singer, carry the bread, and together we all walk up the street to an isolated area. Melchizedek sits and blesses the bread as the followers bow their heads.

"Father, please bless this food that we are about to receive through your provision," prays Melchizedek. He breaks the bread and passes it around. I take a small piece politely even though I am slightly appalled at the number of hands that have touched it.

"What just happened?" I ask.

"The stones were crying out," Melchizedek replies.

My face must have revealed that, in my opinion, my question has yet to be answered.

"Luke." Melchizedek summons a follower to explain.

"Have you heard of Melchizedek? In the Bible?" Luke asks. When I don't answer he continues, "You can read about him in Genesis. He was a priest that Abraham offered a tenth of all his belongings to."

Melchizedek interjects with a question targeted at me, "Who wrestled with Jacob?"

"I don't know the Bible," I respond, offended by the line of questioning.

Elizabeth, a forty-something Englishwoman, hands me a worn-out Bible. "Here take mine," she says. "I have several. You need it more than I do." I accept it and turn to Melchizedek.

"When did you arrive in Israel?" I ask as I start to believe that I may be viewing a sufferer of the Jerusalem syndrome.

"I never left Israel. And although you see me in the physical sense, I am not confined to time," Melchizedek replies with authority.

Elizabeth leans over to me and whispers, "C. S. Lewis explains this really well."

I feel as if I had just walked into another dimension. And frankly, I feel a little scared. "It's getting dark out; I need to head home," I say, standing to excuse myself, with the bread still awkwardly in my hand.

"You're walking away from the light," Melchizedek says.

"It was very interesting to meet you all," I say as I walk quickly away.

The walk home is a blur of unformed thoughts about the surreal experience. I throw the bread to some stray birds as if I am trying to cast away all remnants of the encounter. By the time I reach my apartment, I am fighting away tears of confusion. As I look through my shimmering tears, I see Cohen and Cameron in his doorway saying goodbye. Cameron hugs him as if she never wants to let go. She is truly beautiful. Her skin is so flawless that it seems as though you are looking at her through a soft-focus lens. Her hair is brown with soft curls, and although she has the sides pulled up, the events of the day or the affection from Cohen have freed the soft ringlets, which frame her face.

"We'll see each other soon, Cameron," Cohen says to her over her shoulder as he glances my way. He gives her a quick kiss goodbye. She reluctantly walks away from him as I approach. Cameron also has a tear in her eye but manages to greet me with a smile. I force a smile back, with a frog tight in my throat. I can hardly breathe now.

"Journey," Cohen calls to me. I look away, embarrassed by my emotions.

"Hi," I reply.

"How has your first few days here been?"

"Exhausting." I can't think well enough to lie.

"Would you like to sit on my balcony and talk about it?" I don't know why, but the offer seems so completely inviting. Is it the concern in his voice? The fact that I am in a foreign country without a friend? The depth of concern in his eyes? The fact that what I have just experienced has left me feeling so vulnerable? I nod and fight even harder to stop the tears, unsuccessfully. He ushers me inside, his arm around me as I stammer through his impeccably ordered living space. He offers me a tissue from a box, which I accept. He then asks if I would like a glass of wine. I accept, as I nervously comment on how much I enjoyed the realtor's gift of wine. We walk onto the balcony together. As we step outside, I notice for the first time how full and huge the moon looks. The light defines his strong jawline; his smile softens the canvas.

"So you're a fan of Mount Carmel. Well, I hope you like this." He hands me a glass, as he continues, "How was your experience visiting the Western Wall?"

"Thank you again for catching me," I say, immersed in the memory of my other embarrassing moment with him.

"It was my pleasure," he says. I stare at him for a moment and believe him. He seems to have a hero complex, and it suits him.

I break away from my stare and try to refocus my thoughts, "My experience at the Wall…I was overwhelmed. I thought it was beautiful." I felt the need to say something positive, and it was true.

"But you look upset." His brown eyes catch the light, with the infinity I could get lost in. They search my soul.

"I followed the guy who sang the song." How could I not be honest with such an honest-looking guy.

"The Shema." He clarifies the name of the song.

"What is the song about anyway?"

"Hear, O Israel, the Lord our God, the Lord is One."

For a moment I ponder the words, which seem to provide very little insight. "I followed the guy who sang it. He had these followers, and they called him Melchizedek. And I think he insinuated that he was God in the flesh."

"Was he?"

"I don't know," I say.

He looks at me patiently, as if he is waiting for me to clear up the uncertainty in my own mind.

I succumb to the pressure and feel the need to give more of an answer. "No," I say.

"Do you think if you saw God face to face, that you would recognize Him?"

"That's like asking me if I saw the tooth fairy, would I recognize her?"

Cohen looks at me with compassion for a moment. He holds up his glass for a toast. "L'chaim, to life." He translates his toast for my benefit.

I pick up my glass and toast his. "L'chaim." I take a sip as he touches my back ever so softly. His touch is comforting, appropriate, nonthreatening, and welcome.

"How can you look at this city and not believe?" he asks as he looks out over the city. And the *feeling* of my soul being too big for my body comes over me like a wave once again. I let it wash over me. I somehow feel comfortable not answering Cohen or talking any more at all. We stare out at the city and drink another glass of wine. He is right, this city is at least trying to testify to a god.

If one exists, I may have just felt His warmth, His Spirit again.

The next morning I wake up in my bedroom. The balcony door is open, and the sun is shining in. I hear stray cats fighting somewhere close by. I open my eyes as the fan blows over me. The Muslim loudspeaker is proclaiming God's greatness unbeknownst to me. I stretch my legs on the soft sheets and remember how good Tré's bed felt and try not to think of him now. I walk downstairs and grab a cup of coffee and walk out onto the living room balcony to drink it. I am greeted by the bright sun in the cloudless sky. As I walk outside, I squint the light to see Cohen on his balcony watering plants. I wave hello.

"Good morning," I call out to him.

"Good morning."

"I forgot to ask you something."

"Yes," he replies.

"I was wondering if you know where I could take Israeli martial arts." I am still feverishly trying to check "to-do" items off of Dr. Oberstein's list.

"I can teach you," Cohen says decisively.

"Yeah?"

"Sure."

"Are you any good?" I ask.

"You tell me. When do you want to start?"

"Are you challenging me?"

"Are you up for a challenge?"

"In about an hour?" I ask.

"Why don't you rest and enjoy the Shabbat. Come over when it gets dark outside." I agree, thankfully, but I hate to admit that a little envy swells up in me when I think about how everyone I meet seems to have a spiritual element, interest, or tradition.

In light of experiencing the culture, I release myself from Dr. Oberstein's "to-do" list for the day and rest as Cohen commanded. I must be completely jetlagged because it is no problem to comply with the Shabbat. I lie on the couch and listen to my "stolen" John Mayer CD and try not to think about Tré.

When I arrive on Cohen's doorstep, I am absolutely certain that it is dusk. I lift up my fist to knock on the door but he preemptively opens it with a smile.

"Not a moment too soon," he says.

"Likewise."

"You look rested."

"Yes, I am very rested. Thank you."

"Are you thirsty?"

"I'm fine, thanks. I am a little anxious to get started on my learning. I'm already warmed up." I am a little assertive about learning this new art. Cohen complies with my determination and proceeds with the lesson.

"In Israel, you should be prepared to defend yourself at any time and in any place." That's about as much verbal instruction as he gives me. He comes up behind me and grabs my arms. I resort to typical karate release.

"Forget everything you know about karate. Feel and anticipate," he says.

He was serious and he knew what he was talking about. He quickly moved closer and put me in another hold. He released me and motioned for me to repeat his move. He moved through several new holds, released me, and then I repeated them. It wasn't long before I seemed to anticipate him, and we began to spar intensely. He found reflexes and pressure points, I didn't even know existed. As much as I fought, I knew that every cell in my body was subservient to him. And there was no doubt in my mind that he knew it too.

He smelt like his clothes had been washed in baby detergent and hung on the line. There was a clean scent about him. I liked that he didn't talk much. He communicated a lot through his eyes and maneuvering my body into the moves that he would want me to learn. And although his hands were all over my body, I, for some reason, trusted him. Israeli martial arts is aggressive, close combat, and downright dirty fighting, and he somehow taught me with dignity and respect. And even in this first lesson, there were moments when I could get lost in the concentration of it, and I needed that.

Time lost all meaning and by the time we actually stopped, we were both dripping in sweat.

"You had enough?" he asks.

"For today," I say, embarrassingly breathless.

"What do you think?"

"Good workout. Good teacher. When can we do it again?" I sound pathetically tired.

"Anytime."

I lean against the bar to catch my breath. "Where do you work?"

"You know the new hotel they're building near the cinematheque?"

"The lavish hotel?" I can't help recalling it. The architecture makes a mockery of the Taj Mahal.

"Yes, I work construction on that."

"So in the evenings I guess you're pretty tired, huh?"

"I'll save some energy for your cause."

...

I came back the very next day. You know I did.

As I walk over to his house for my next lesson, I can smell dinner from outside. As I approach the doorway, I hear him call from the kitchen, "Please come in." Inside, the smell is more than inviting.

"The food smells great," I say.

"It's still cooking. I thought we would spar first."

"Is Cameron coming over?"

"Not today."

"She's beautiful," I say, more to pry about their relationship than just to point out the truth that it is.

"She has a beautiful soul." His insight cuts through my superficial comment. "She owns and runs an orphanage." Cohen smiles warmly at me.

The pride I feel for my own profession feels upstaged by this woman's heart. How rare physical beauty and humanity are in one person. She is interesting, but Cohen is even more interesting. I have to know and dare to ask, "Have you two been together very long?"

"We're not romantically involved."

"It looks like you are."

"She is affectionate, and so am I."

He approaches me and puts his hand on my face. From the sparring the previous day, we seem to be losing our need for the normal parameters of body space. He looks intently into my eyes, his forehead touches mine. I almost forget what we are talking about.

"She understands me…and isn't that our deepest desire…to be understood?"

My soul groaned within me. He had just articulated my heart's desire, the itch I couldn't scratch, the truth I couldn't lie about, and obviously the secret I couldn't hide. He had a way of asking questions that I couldn't bring myself to answer so I basically treated them all like they were rhetorical. I ended my own silence by trying to put him in a hold.

Cohen put me flat on my back. We continued to spar.

I asked about Cameron not because I was interested in Cohen romantically. Don't get me wrong; I was jealous of Cameron with Cohen. I was jealous of the way he looked at her and touched her. Cohen had a beautiful body, and he was attractive inside and out. And there was definitely a chemistry between us, but it wasn't quite physical.

By the time we finished the lesson, my muscles shook from fatigue, and my stomach ached from insatiable hunger. Dinner was so incredibly good, I ate ravenously without shame. "This ministered to me," I confessed without

49

forethought. What a strange grouping of words, I thought, and ones I had never used together. I wasn't worried about how I looked, or what to say, or whether I wasn't being polite. I just *was* with Cohen, and I allowed him to teach me and take care of me. He insisted that I not help with dishes, and sent me home with all the leftovers. There was no awkward goodbye, just an arrangement for a future lesson.

Chapter Four

I take a deep cleansing breath before entering the psychiatric unit at Kfar Shaul Hospital in the morning. Yonathan walks up to shake my hand and looks genuinely happy to see me.

"Journey, how are you? We thought you'd come in early when you heard about the Wailing Wall," he says.

"Heard? I was there." I smile back proudly. I am well aware that it has made international news.

"Did you see the man?" he asks.

"Yes, and I followed him."

Yonathan escorts me to Dr. Oberstein's office again. Dr. Oberstein is having a cigar at his desk with an older gentleman, whose nose is red from what I can only presume is years of drinking too much alcohol. Dr. Oberstein smiles at me and beckons me into the room, waving his cigar toward himself.

"Yes, it's a nonsmoking hospital but they allow me certain privileges. Journey, this is Dr. Beckerman, our consulting statistician."

"Nice to meet you. How long have you had this gambling problem?" I ask slyly.

"What?" Dr. Oberstein looks a little confused at my joke.

"It's a joke. Statisticians are known gamblers. And of course I do my share for the economy," Dr. Beckerman says, as he clears his throat and smiles.

"Journey was at the Western Wall during the excitement," says Yonathan.

"What did you see?" Dr. Oberstein leans forward in interest.

"I was there when he sang, and I followed him."

"Did you get a picture?"

"No."

"Make sure you get her a camera today," Dr. Oberstein says to Yonathan. Then he addresses the group as a whole, "I can't believe the news coverage didn't have any real-time photos or video."

"It was too chaotic...too compelling," I say. "I saw the news media pass by him after he had sung."

"What was your impression? Was it a quake? Was there a strong wind?" Dr. Oberstein asks.

"I don't know. This man sang supernaturally loud and strong. There were a lot of people there. Could there have been some sort of natural amphitheater effect? There was definitely a wind." I try to explain the unexplainable and feel more than inept.

"You think the vibrations from his voice allowed for the loosening of the prayers?" Dr. Oberstein continues his investigation.

"I can only guess."

"People say it was beautiful." Dr. Oberstein waves his cigar around as he speaks. I realize that he is no longer concerned about a rational explanation. Since he is not wearing a kippah, I have no reference for his religious tenets, but his eyes sparkle with inspiration.

"It was," I say, meeting his eyes, hoping to reflect the same truthful interest.

"I'm jealous, and this was just your first day in Israel. What about the man? Do you believe that he had the Jerusalem syndrome?" Dr. Oberstein's interest now narrows on his profession.

"He wouldn't admit to just arriving," I answer, knowing the criteria for the diagnosis.

"Who did he claim to be?" Dr. Oberstein asks, testing my knowledge of the other criteria.

"His followers called him Melchizedek."

"What did he say?" Dr. Oberstein leans into his question.

"He asked me who I thought wrestled with Jacob."

Dr. Oberstein is thoroughly excited, all but salivating, "A Christophany. This would be unusual for the Jerusalem syndrome. We get a lot of John the Baptists, and King Davids and Jesus Christs. But this man claims to be enigmatic historical figures that are mentioned ever so briefly in the Torah…the Bible, and theologians argue whether they are God incarnate. This man is claiming to be the physical presence of God."

Yonathan reads my puzzled look and tries to explain further, "Christophany, theophany, it's a matter of semantics. They are words that describe the appearance of God in physical form as He appears to individuals, not as the Messiah, or Jesus Christ. He isn't there to fulfill prophecy. He doesn't introduce Himself as God. He is there to build the faith of individuals. He enters the timeline of humanity because He is God and He is taking the liberty to do so."

I look over at the statistician. "What are the chances of this man appearing and singing like that and the prayers falling by natural causes?" I ask, wanting to be a team player.

"Your question is beyond the scope of my abilities, but my gut tells me that the simultaneous occurrences are remarkable," he answers.

"Remarkable" is another word for "statistically significant." These are intellectuals who are not afraid to consider the spiritual. I am starting to feel like I can't hang with these people. I am used to scientists who refute anything that is not objective. But this is Israel. And I wonder, for the briefest moment, whether my sense of the *feeling* would be considered subjective or objective.

Dr. Oberstein puts out his cigar, "Your assignment today," he says, "go find Melchizedek and bring him to me. You can take Yonathan with you." I leave the office with Yonathan. I feel as though I have just been infected with Dr. Oberstein's excitement. The man loves his work.

...

Cameron walks up to the construction site of the hotel near the cinematheque. Her natural highlights glisten in the noonday sun. She looks around and approaches one of the workers.

"Shalom," she says in greeting.

"Shalom," he replies.

The two continue their conversation in Hebrew. "Excuse me, but I am looking for Cohen," Cameron says. The foreman stops his work completely, captivated by her looks. She is dressed in a simple white embroidered dress. The kind they sell in the Old City when they talk down their own price and offer a special one "for you."

"There's his foreman." The construction worker gestures to another hardhat worker. Cameron walks over to him. He smiles at her, and he also is unable to complete his work, taken back by her beauty. She smiles back, revealing a deep dimple in her cheek. She is a breathtaking Israeli woman who is seemingly unaware of her own beauty.

"Shalom," she says.

The foreman speaks to her in their native language, "Hello. You must be Cameron."

"Yes."

"Well, I was beginning to think I'd never meet you."

Cameron smiles, unsure what he means.

"I've got six of Cohen's paychecks made out to you. He never wanted the paychecks put in his name, and when you got someone as

talented and hardworking as Cohen, you make allowance," the foreman says.

Cameron looks surprised at his statement. The foreman walks Cameron over to the onsite office trailer, which he enters. She stands at the doorway.

"Is Cohen here?"

The foreman thumbs through some checks. "Cohen is expecting you. He's taking a lunch today in the park over there. He asked me to invite you to join him." He finds her checks. "Cameron Abramson."

Cameron smiles, a little amused, "Yes."

He hands her the checks. "You and Cohen take as long of a lunch as you like. He deserves a break; he's a hard worker," he says.

Cameron smiles again and thanks him. She takes the short walk over to the park and sees Cohen sitting on a blanket. The foreman's eyes can't help but follow her until she is out of sight. As she approaches, Cohen stands up and gives her a hug and a kiss.

"So you have your down payment," he nods toward the checks.

"Yes. Thank you. I've already called the realtor you suggested," she says.

"I brought lunch," he says.

She sits down with him and ignores the lunch for now. They embrace, and soon they are lying on their backs looking up at the sky. Cohen points toward the sky, whispering something in her ear. He smiles as he looks at her.

"Right there," he adds.

"Where?" Cameron laughs, searching the sky.

Cohen points again. "I can't make you see."

"Right now I would rather look at you." She turns to him and touches his face. She leans against him. He touches her face. "You know how much I needed you now?" Her question is a statement.

"I'll always provide for you one way or another. You don't need to worry about that. You're my baby." He kisses her forehead. She rests her face against his, their fingers intertwined.

...

I walk past the park where Cohen and Cameron are lying on the blanket. Yonathan walks with me, as we search for Melchizedek. Although I can see Cohen and Cameron, the jealous pit in my stomach doesn't allow me to be friendly. Besides, they look like they are enjoying the moment together, alone.

Yonathan, unaware of the reason for my distraction, attempts to gain my attention. "So your position is actually a grant from the hospital and the office of tourism. The Jerusalem syndrome ends up costing Israel a lot of money for the hospitalizations, and oftentimes we have to fly the patients back to their families at our expense," he says as part of my orientation.

"And what is the usual prognosis, in your opinion?" I try to regain focus.

"If there is no prior history of psychotic episodes, they make a complete recovery in five to ten days."

"So do you think we will know about Melchizedek in five to ten days?" I ask.

"If he does have the Jerusalem syndrome, it may be a more difficult case because, from what you said, he has followers, and with the dramatic events that unfolded at the Wall, these factors could reinforce the delusions."

We continue walking down the street, and I assume that Yonathan is filling the time with polite conversation. "Are you trying to make Aliyah?" he asks.

The word, obviously Hebrew, was Greek to me. I was so naïve about Jewish culture that I can only imagine that my response must have seemed rude.

"What?" I ask.

"Aliyah," he repeats.

"No, I don't think so. I am not familiar with that term."

He doesn't explain it but looks less interested in me as a person.

Later, I learn that Aliyah is gaining citizenship to Israel, through the Law of Return. My simple answer spoke volumes about my faith, my long-term career aspirations in Israel, and any possible future romantic relationship with him, if that was ever a thought in his mind. Then again, maybe he was just making conversation.

Yonathan points to a woman who is standing facing the street, draped in colorful fabric. She is swaying back and forth with her eyes closed. Yonathan approaches her and I follow.

"Shalom," he says to her. The lady just smiles and continues swaying to nonexistent music. I slowly approach her and speak in English.

"Hi, how are you?" I ask.

The lady looks at me and touches my arm. "I'm just enjoying the city my son was born in," she says with a thick Southern accent.

"Oh, who's your son?" I ask.

"You know who...Jesus." She smiles, and looks at me almost as though she knows that she is saying something a little off.

"How long have you been in the city?" I try to establish a time frame.

"Oh, I don't know."

I try to ask it another way. "Were you on a plane recently?"

"Yes, I was."

Yonathan asks her, "Are you here with family or friends?"

"Well, I was here with a group of nice people, but they didn't want to stay here, and I did. So, I just let them go."

"Are you hungry?" I ask. She looks famished, and her lips are chapped and dry. In a strange contrast, sweat beads form linear rows above her lip, like the old-school candy buttons on paper tape. The sun has burned her fair face, and there are several sun blisters on her forehead. Her hair is wet with sweat and has formed unplanned dreads, from where it looks like it hasn't been brushed in days.

"I've been fasting, but I'm about done with that now."

"Well, we were about to go back to our work and have some lunch. Would you like to join us?" I ask, forcing a very convincing Southern accent.

"That might be nice. This sun is getting awfully hot."

I hand her an unopened water bottle from my bag. She opens it and drinks half of the bottle.

We arrive safely at Kfar Shaul Hospital with little fanfare. I sit with "Mary" in the dayroom. Yonathan walks just beyond the Plexiglas doors to speak with Dr. Oberstein and his nurse. They are already engaged in conversation.

"He's probably a genius," says Dr. Oberstein. "He appears to know more Scripture than most American preachers. And apparently he has quite a voice."

"Still talking about Melchizedek?" Yonathan interrupts.

"Of course." Dr. Oberstein smiles and greets Yonathan with a manly, parental squeeze on the shoulder. Dr. Oberstein takes one look over into the dayroom and redirects his focus, "What do we have here?" he says looking over at me and Mary sitting on the couch.

"The Virgin Mary, who thinks Jesus was born in Jerusalem," Yonathan replies.

"Then I shall sing 'O Little Town of Bethlehem' to her," he says in a forced baritone. It is obvious he loves his work.

"She's from the Deep South. No information on family. No sample yet," Yonathan reports.

Dr. Oberstein extends his hand to the nurse, who is ready with supplies for a blood sample: a thin rubber tourniquet, alcohol, a needle, and several vials. His eyes assess me, as well has Mary, before he calmly asks Yonathan, "How was Journey?"

"She was great," he says.

Dr. Oberstein walks into the room where Mary and I are seated.

"Hello, and who do we have here?" he asks her.

Mary looks to me for support and encouragement.

"He's a friend," I whisper to her.

"Mary," she answers.

I catch Yonathan's eye through the Plexiglas. He casually motions for me to come out of the room.

"Did you enjoy your food?" Dr. Oberstein asks Mary.

Mary nods.

"Please excuse me," I say, as I walk out.

Dr. Oberstein continues with Mary, "Would you like anything else? How about some banana pudding?"

Just outside the dayroom I approach Yonathan and the nurse.

"What's up?" I ask.

"Sorry, I know you would probably like to observe, but Dr. Oberstein wants to get a blood sample," he says.

"But she is so adamant about not giving one," I say.

"Did he offer her banana pudding?" the nurse inquires, as if he had just ordered an X-ray.

"Yes," I say, impressed.

The nurse walks quickly away.

"We are probably the only place in all of Israel that serves banana pudding. If you want to identify with a group of people," says Yonathan, "eat their food and speak their language. That's why Dr. Oberstein thought it was important

59

to hire an American for your position. Most of our patients are from the States."

Yonathan points to Mary through the Plexiglas. I can see Mary putting out her arm, willingly, as Dr. Oberstein places the tourniquet on it.

"What did he say to her?" I ask.

"No one knows. No one likes getting blood drawn, and we've had some very resistant patients. But he always comes out with a sample…always the first stick…and always alone."

"That's impressive," I say.

Dr. Oberstein walks out of the dayroom with the filled blood vials.

"That's Dr. Oberstein," Yonathan says with a smile as he joins us.

The nurse returns with the banana pudding. Dr. Oberstein hands her two vials of blood.

"Routine labs," he says to her.

Dr. Oberstein hands me a vial and says, "Genetic markers." The nurse hands Dr. Oberstein the banana pudding, and he walks back into the dayroom whistling "O Little Town of Bethlehem."

I go to the lab to observe the sample of blood that I have been given. I look through the lens of the elaborate genetic testing equipment and then pull away and blink in unbelief. I take a second look, as if that would somehow change the results that I have just seen. I document my findings, and then I walk down to Dr. Oberstein's office. He sits at his desk with dictation equipment in his hand.

"Medical history, unremarkable at this time. Consult to Dr. Lieberman. Genetic consult to Dr. Kaufmann," he says in Hebrew. I recognize only my name but assume he is referring to the consult. He pushes a button on his equipment to pause.

"No genetic markers for psychosis," I report.

"Then our research begins. Good work, Journey. Yonathan is off tomorrow. How do you feel about looking for Melchizedek alone?

"Fine," I lied. What choice did I have? Melchizedek unravels my threads, but the last thing I want to do is make the man feel like he made a mistake by hiring me.

"Are you sure?" He looks at me for more certainty.

"Yes," I insist. I am fully aware that I am lying to probably the best psychiatrist in the world.

"Your safety comes first." Dr. Oberstein's words take on parental concern. "Have you looked into the Israeli martial arts?"

"I've begun training."

"Good." He gives a satisfied nod. He pushes a button on his dictating device and rambles on in Hebrew, "Genetic markers for psychosis, negative."

I turn to leave as he resumes his work. I hear him push the button to stop.

"Journey?" he calls. I stop at his door.

"Yes, Dr. Oberstein." I turn toward him.

"Some of my most challenging patients have been the most brilliant. This is what we as physicians do: We rise to the challenge." As he speaks, he gestures with all four fingers touching his thumb, his palm toward himself, in a gesture that looks more Italian than anything else. He continues, "In helping others, we learn about ourselves, and this can be the most difficult part of our work."

I let out the breath I have been holding in. I bite my lip as if that, in and of itself, has revealed too much. He smiles.

There is no doubt in my mind that he is a good psychiatrist. His truth has politely exposed my lie.

"Thank you," I say, thankful to be working with such an insightful and thoughtful man.

After my first workday, I climb onto Bus 14 to make my way home. I sit down beside a religious man who gets up and takes another seat. I admit I get a little offended. In Israel, what I call a religious man is one who is dressed in a black hat, black pants, and a long black jacket and usually, interestingly enough, smoking a cigarette on the street, an obvious privilege God must have left as a grey area in the Torah just for them. For I feel certain they have checked the law. I move into the seat he just left and look out the window as the bus continues on. It stops again. Tré enters, hands the bus driver a bus ticket, and walks towards me. I can't breathe and can't believe my eyes. He sits down beside me, and I try to play it cool.

"Of all the buses, on all the routes, in all of Jerusalem, he walks onto mine." I speak my own narration with my half-ripped-off *Casablanca* line.

Tré smiles and looks genuinely happy to see me. "I love Humphrey Bogart," he says, letting me know that he actually got my joke.

"Are you sure you want to sit here?" I ask.

"Why?"

"Well, apparently I stink," I say a little louder than necessary, half hoping the religious man will hear. Tré looks confused, but he inhales through his nose in my direction, anyway.

"You don't stink."

"Every time I get on a bus and sit down, the person I sit beside gets up and takes another seat," I try to explain.

Tré laughs and whispers, "Did you sit beside a religious man?"

"I took the first seat..." I think for a moment then answer, "Yes."

Tré leans over to me and whispers again, "A religious man won't sit beside a woman who is not his wife."

I can't help but let my thoughts segue from the conversation for a moment. It is so good to feel close to him again. With his mouth near my ear I gaze forward and can only think that this is beyond a temptation. How am I supposed to respond to this? It's not fair. Say something. I remember that I am having a conversation and hope that it's not too late to still comment.

"You're kidding... What if it was the last seat?" I turn to look at him and see his pale eyes that look honeydew melon today.

"He'd stand," he says matter-of-factly but smiles and looks at my mouth. I smile too, but what would have seemed more appropriate would be to kiss him, and to forget that we are on a bus filled with people, not to mention the religious man, and that we have two sad goodbyes between us already because my beliefs don't reflect his. Anticipating that this goodbye is due to be less dramatic, I point to the next stop.

"This is my stop." The bus comes to a halt. Tré stands up to let me out. I can't bear to look at him. I slide by and turn to leave him. He takes hold of my hand firmly and follows me out. We hold hands on the walk home as the clouds look magnificently full. As we approach the steps to my door, he stops short and pulls tension between our hands, suggesting another goodbye.

I had started to assume something more...coffee, at the very least.

"You just came to walk me home?" I say, sensing hesitation.

Tré nods apologetically.

I look away and shake my head disappointedly. I feel tears threaten and hope that he can't yet see them. "Thank you." I manage to be polite. We stare at each other for a moment. It starts to rain.

Tré looks up in disbelief and smiles. "It's raining. This is the first time it has rained since I've been here," he says.

I had no idea how rare rain is in Jerusalem this time of year. It was practically a miracle.

"It's good to see you smile," I say, forgetting my pain, remembering his recent hurt. It actually begins to pour and the weight of the rain makes some of my hair fall in my eyes. He moves it away, and again it seems as if the gesture is too hard for him to resist. He begins to kiss me.

If ever there were a song that could capture a moment in time, I don't think that any could do it better than John Mayer's song, "Edge of Desire." To this day I can't hear it without thinking about those moments. There is nothing like kissing in the pouring rain.

Every cell in his body was searching and every cell in mine was being found. The cool rain made the warmth of his body feel even more inviting. There was no thought of the neighbors. I was oblivious to the sound of the tires of a car on the wet road passing by. We didn't care about the sea of theological differences between us at that moment. We were not two intellectuals, we were two people ruled by an innate desire and a chemistry so strong we couldn't possibly overcome it. There was only Tré and me. With the rain pounding on our skin, we forgot ourselves.

And for the moment and the rest of the night, it seems as though we tried to forget God… if that's even possible.

We move through the front door still kissing. Clothes cascade to the floor as we make our way into the shower, and then on to the bedroom.

As he lies on top of me, he breaks away from kissing me to look at me and offer what is chivalrously becoming a ritual moment of questioning my certainty of continuing on. I close my eyes and pull him toward me, inviting him back.

...

I open my eyes in the morning and hear the sound of stray cats fighting, Jerusalem's unrelenting alarm clock. The fan blows over me, and I find that Tré's arms are still wrapped around me, his face half-buried in my hair. He is still asleep. I carefully move away from him and look ever so briefly at his handsome face. With his eyes closed, he looks so sweet. I want to stay in bed with him all day, but I am afraid the morning might bring regret for Tré. And if it does, I am going to need some coffee.

I am standing on the living room balcony, leaning slightly over the railing, drinking my cup of slow-roasted courage, when Tré comes out holding his cup of coffee. He has a serious look on his face. He puts his free hand around my waist and gives me a little kiss on the shoulder. We look out at the city together.

"Thank you for the coffee," he says.

"You're welcome. Thank you for walking me home."

"That's really all I intended to do." Here it comes. I brace myself for the words that follow. "Journey, I'm sorry."

I'm hurt. I'm mad. I want to tell him that's the last thing I want to hear. But is there really any point in that? I try to joke, "Oh really? When can I expect you to be sorry again?" It doesn't go over very well.

"I should go," he says politely.

Tré and I walk out of my rental. I stand in my doorway and accept my kiss goodbye. Cohen is leaving his house at the same time. He looks our way, but we don't look his. Tré heads down the street behind Cohen, leaving me in the doorway, very alone.

•••

Tré steps on Bus 14 and takes out his bus ticket, which has practically dissolved from the rain. It is totally illegible. He searches in his pocket for money.

The bus driver interrupts Tré's useless attempts to find payment and says, "The passenger before you paid for you." Tré stares at the bus driver for a moment and then looks through the bus to see Cohen. Tré walks further onto the bus.

"Thank you," Tré says to Cohen in Hebrew.

"You're welcome," Cohen replies in the same language.

Tré walks past the open seat beside Cohen and takes a seat at the back of the bus.

•••

Cameron takes a step out of the realtor's car in northern Israel. The realtor opens a squeaky door to the house, and shows her around the property, which seems dirty and poorly built. It is empty except for a carved piece of wood that hangs on the wall with the inscription: Deuteronomy 33:24. Cameron and the realtor speak to one another in Hebrew.

"Are you sure this is the right place?" Cameron asks desperately.

"This is the address you gave me."

"Who lived here?"

"This was not exactly a home. It housed Israeli oil drillers at one time. This is a beautiful piece of land. You have a ninety-nine-year lease…most of the appraised value is for the lease on the land. You are in the country, so you can build another home as big as you want. There is plenty of room for a swing set, for the children to run and play. You are using this property for an orphanage, am I right?"

"Yes. How are the utilities?"

"It has electricity. There is well water, but it is good only for running the toilet."

"What about drinking and bathing, and laundry?" Cameron asks, more than frustrated.

"Laundry, yes. Drinking and bathing, no. You will need a deeper well; the metals and bacteria register too high. It will probably cost you at least $2,000."

"We have to be out of our orphanage by the end of the week," Cameron shakes her head in disappointment. *"I'll take it,"* she says through her teeth.

...

I am walking down Emek Rafiem Street when I see Melchizedek on the other side of the road. He helps a lady with a stroller get on a bus but doesn't get on himself. I stop to observe him and collect myself. Then, I approach him.

"Melchizedek?"

"You can call me that," he says as he continues walking.

"I met you the other night after you sang."

"I remember you."

"Are you hungry?"

"If I were hungry, I wouldn't tell you."

I realize that there is a pizza restaurant in front us. I am looking around searching for something, anything, to say when I see Aki walking toward us on the other side of the street. He seems to be looking around casually, but he doesn't spot us.

"The man who tried to have you arrested is walking on the other side of the street. Would you like to have a slice of pizza with me?"

He gestures for me to enter first and follows me into the pizza restaurant.

"I'm going to have a slice; would you like one?" I ask.

"No."

I watch as Aki passes our area. He is still on the other side of the street. I now realize that his eyes calculate every detail of his surroundings. How we manage to escape his surveying eyes is baffling. I then notice that the pizza shop worker is staring at me, waiting for me to order.

"Do you speak English?"

"What would you like?" he asks in English.

"I'll have one slice of pizza." I look up at the board of different kinds of pizza toppings that are listed.

"Do you have bacon and mushrooms?" I ask. The cook smiles and shakes his head, uncomprehending.

Melchizedek leans toward me and quietly and nonchalantly states, "This is a kosher restaurant. They don't put pork or any kind of meat on pizza."

I want to crawl under the table. My only salvation is that I don't think that the worker understood the word "bacon" in English.

"I'll have a slice of cheese, please," I say sheepishly.

Melchizedek sits and waits with me. Surprisingly few people are in the shop.

"I work with a hospital that helps people who come here and feel a bit…overwhelmed…Do you think that you might like to go there with me?" I ask him.

"Do I look overwhelmed?"

He honestly doesn't. He looks clean and calm.

"Do you think that it would be possible, if you are who you say that you are, that I could get a sample of your blood?"

"Why?"

"I'm a geneticist, and I could test your blood."

"For what?"

"Maybe it's possible for your blood to help others." I'm not lying to him, I'm still telling the truth, but I'm trying to speak within what would make sense through the veil of his alleged delusions.

"My blood has already been shed once and for all, to help others," he replies.

I take out my camera. I have to come back to the hospital with something.

"Could I at least get a picture?"

"This generation is always looking for proof…when it's everywhere." At that Melchizedek walks out of the restaurant. I don't follow him. I sit and ponder his statements, his demeanor…his reality.

•••

I sit in Dr. Oberstein's office and report that I have spotted Melchizedek. Yonathan stands up and explodes. "Why didn't you follow him?"

"I thought it might offend him?" I say in my defense.

"No. She did the right thing. She is establishing rapport," Dr. Oberstein says in his comforting way.

"I thought you were off," I say to Yonathan, a little perturbed that he would challenge my decision.

"I got called in. Our census is high since his…appearance," he replies.

"Did he say anything else? Did anything seem out of character for this…Christophany?" Dr. Oberstein inquires with intrigue.

"Well, I was a little offended when he said, 'If I were hungry, I wouldn't tell you.'"

Yonathan chimes in again to finish the Scripture quote, "…for the world is mine, and all that is in it. Psalm 50:12."

Dr. Oberstein says excitedly, "This guy is not only well read, he *thinks* with Scripture. He doesn't speak Hebrew that you've seen except the Shema, and he has Christian beliefs, in that he talked about the shedding of blood. Good work, Journey."

"Thank you."

"Would you mind heading to the lab? There are two samples waiting for you," Dr. Oberstein says as he lights a cigar.

In the lab, I look through the lens of my testing equipment, then make a few notes on paper. Dr. Oberstein stops at the door; I feel his presence and look up.

"What's the score?"

"One to one," I say, following up his metaphor.

"The male had the markers?" he asks presumptuously.

I nod in affirmation.

"Why don't you work in the field tomorrow?" he instructs.

"Sure."

"Have a good night."

"Good night."

Dr. Oberstein starts to walk away, then turns back toward me, in accordance with his one-last thing-routine. "Oh, and Journey?"

"Yes."

"We don't need Melchizedek for our research, and he doesn't sound like a threat to others. He seems to be able to care for himself...I'm just fascinated by him."

I smile, "Me too."

Chapter Five

I walk into Cohen's living room, and there is a queen-sized mattress on the floor. I just look at it, all out of place.

"That's nice, Cohen, but I really don't feel that way about you," I say jokingly to him, but my words are very true. I assume that the mattress is needed for our martial arts lesson.

"Oh, I'm glad you said that because I don't feel that way about you, either," he says softly, in a comforting way.

"Seriously?" I ask.

"Seriously," he affirms.

I let out a sigh of relief, accidentally. Glad that was as much of *that* conversation as we needed to have.

"Now that we've got that cleared up," he continues, "can you greet me with a traditional Israeli hug and kiss?"

I hold out my arms gladly and step into his true, heartfelt embrace. He gives me a kiss on the cheek.

"Thank you, I really needed that," I say. Then I pick up the large cutting knife that he has on the table. I walk towards him and say, "Now show me what the mattress is for." I am excited about the next lesson.

In a second he has me on the mattress with the knife at my back. He lets me up, holds the knife blade towards me, and I repeat his previous moves. Eventually, the knife is forgone and we continue to spar. Everything is going well, and there are times when I would swear that we are defying gravity, or space, or time. Then, somewhere between concentrating on the lesson and being lost in the rhythm of the art, as I move with Cohen, the *feeling* rushes over me, as if my soul was once again welling up with a tingly warmth that dared my body to hold it in. I look at Cohen and wonder if he felt it too. I start to lose concentration at this point. It is clear I am off my mark.

"What are you thinking about?" he asks.

I sit down on the mattress Indian-style. He sits down the same way and looks intently into my eyes.

"It's nothing."

"You can tell me anything," he says.

"What do you think about carbon-14 dating?" I ask.

He doesn't miss a beat at the untimely question. "How old did a tree look when it was one day old? Or how old did Adam look when he was one day old? The Earth, when it was created, had an appearance of age."

He addressed the core of my question completely, and he had a point there, as far as the theory of creation goes, that I had never thought about.

"Where were you when I was taking eighth-grade science?" I ask lightly, but I am still thinking much deeper.

"Around." He smiles.

As I sat there, I couldn't help but imagine what we looked like from a distance. I thought there might be something poetic about our silhouettes focused on each other against the dissipating light of the city, which shined through the glass balcony doors.

•••

I am walking down Jaffa Street when I spot a forty-something-year-old gentleman, whom we'll call J. S. Prophet. He is sitting in front of the Bible store.

"Behold, a voice in the night sayeth, 'I am the way,'" he says with a Southern accent. I sit down on the curb beside him and look at him.

"You like banana pudding?" I ask him.

···

Before you know it, we are walking down the halls of Kfar
Shaul Hospital.

"Behold, the lights in this building are not true lights," he
says.

I hand two vials to the nurse and keep one for myself.
"Routine labs. Banana pudding STAT," I order jokingly.

Dr. Oberstein walks up. "What do we have here?" he
inquires.

"Your garden-variety prophet from Louisiana, to Newark,
to Tel Aviv; yesterday. Here alone, but has family." I hand
over the family's telephone number.

Dr. Oberstein is beaming with pride over his new
employee.

Later, Dr. Oberstein comes to the door of the lab as I am
documenting my findings.

He presents his familiar question: "What's the score?"

"No markers on him or the other admit," I say. "Admit"
is a term used to refer to someone who is newly admitted to
the hospital.

"Good work," he says as he walks out.

···

It is late in the evening when I open my front door to find
Tré. I don't say anything. He is already breathing fast, and I
know what the look on his face is a precursor to. In a
millisecond, we are engaged in a passionate kiss.

···

I awaken to the infamous Muslim call to prayer over the
loudspeaker. I stretch my legs, feeling the sheets. I reach for
Tré, and find that he is not in bed. Just then, he enters the
doorway with two cups of coffee.

"What are they saying anyway?" I ask, confident he will
know.

73

"'God is great, God is great, God is great,' in Arabic," he replies.

"No cats? Where are the cats?" I question the absence of my morning sound effects. Just then, we hear two cats fighting. Tré laughs a little. I sit up and accept the coffee he offers. He sits beside me on the bed and looks into my eyes.

"I love your brown eye and your green eye," he says.

"It's about time you noticed."

"I noticed when we were on the plane. I just had a lot on my mind."

He made a good point. I pause for a moment and then change the subject. "I want to talk to you about something."

"What's that?" He looks interested and not the slightest bit threatened.

"The *feeling* that you talked about, the first night we were together in New York…God's Spirit…Can you still feel it?"

"No." Tré thinks for a moment. "Not since my father's…no…not since we talked about it."

"You felt it at that moment?" I ask.

"Yes."

"I did, too."

Tré smiles.

I continue my confession. "And I've felt it since then. You might feel like I am pulling you away from God, but I feel like you're bringing me closer."

Maybe I said the right thing. In any event, his escape route wasn't a straight shot. Before long, though, he kisses me goodbye at the door. I close the door, ritualistically refusing to watch him walk away from me.

···

As Tré leaves for work, Cohen is leaving his house too, on cue. Tré accidently catches Cohen's watchful eye.

"Shalom," Tré says dutifully.

"Shalom," Cohen responds genuinely.

Tré crosses the street early as Cohen continues on his side of the street, undoubtedly on the same route leaving the neighborhood. As they reach the corner, the Arab girl from the next street, the one who had thrown the rock at my taxi, steps onto their street.

"Shalom," she calls in Hebrew, not her first language.

"Shalom," Cohen calls back in a truly heartfelt tone.

He continues to walk past her. She picks up rocks off the ground. She throws one at Cohen, who turns instinctively to catch it. The little girl stands there petrified, as Cohen walks over to her and kneels down to look into her eyes. He speaks to her in perfect Arabic, "You have a strong arm....Use it for good." He hands her the rock, her mouth still open in shock, and she drops the rock from her other hand. "Peace," he says in Arabic.

She looks kindly at him for the briefest moment. "Daddy!" She yells in Arabic, in Cohen's face, and then runs back towards her street. Tré looks back to see the sight of the little girl running from where Cohen is still kneeling.

...

Later, while I am working and walking down a Jerusalem street, a man runs past me and grabs my breast. Instinctively, I grab his hand and twist his arm. I use an elbow strike on his arm and hear it crack. I broke his arm before I even thought about what happened. And when I did...think...I let go of him. He yelled and ran away. I didn't chase after him.

An Israeli policeman runs up to me. "Stay here. I will be back," he says in Hebrew. I stay in place, obeying his hand gesture. The Israeli policeman runs quickly after the perpetrator. He calls out on his radio while he is running. He returns minutes later to find me sitting on the bench. He says something again in Hebrew that I don't understand.

"Do you speak English?" I ask.

"I thought you were Israeli. We didn't catch him. Did you get a look at his face?" The police officer asks in English.

"No," I admit.

"Neither did I. That's a problem."

I am baffled and clearly upset by the events. Moreover, I can't believe that this could happen in daylight.

"Is there anything wrong with my shirt?" I say typical victim–style.

The policeman looks at my shirt.

"No. It's a good shirt. It's a nice shirt," he insists. "What's your name?

"Journey."

"Journey, how long have you been in Israel?"

"Not quite a week."

"I am so sorry that this happened. We do have a problem with this. But I hope that you are able to feel safe here, in Israel." He points to the tops of the buildings. I look to see security guards standing up on top of the buildings.

"You see the security up there. We are watching to keep you safe. The crime rate in Israel does not compare to the crime rate in U.S. big cities. It's much, much smaller."

I nod.

"At that, I will leave you. Okay?"

"Yes."

"You are a strong woman. You can obviously defend yourself," he says sternly.

"Thank you."

...

I am just in view of Kfar Shaul Hospital when I see a grey-haired black gentleman walking down the street. He is wearing a sports jacket with the spare button still hanging from the seam in the arm pit.

"Shalom," I say to him.

76

"Shalom and hello to you," he replies back.

"Are you new to Israel?"

"I may be new to Israel, but Israel is old to me," he says with character and an old Southern drawl. I notice one eye is discolored blue and not aligned with the other, suggesting blindness in the one.

"How long have you been here exactly?" I hold to my routine.

"Long enough to make prayers come out the Wall. Did you see it?" he asks proudly.

"Yes....you did that?" I attempt to clarify.

"Right when my foot hit the surface of the platform to the Wall, the prayers fell."

"When the man sang the Shema?" I ask.

"The Shema...like he knew who I was," he says with even more attitude.

"Who are you?"

"I'm Blessed."

"Are you hungry?"

...

I walk onto the psychiatric floor with "Blessed" and three vials of his blood. I hand two to the nurse and keep one for myself. If I can get the blood in the field, I always opt for that so at least I have something to bring back for our research. Crazy people are unpredictable, and I am always afraid they might decide to make a getaway. So far, I've been able to usher all of them in, except of course for our elusive Melchizedek.

"I'm Blessed like when I was in Italy, and I needed clothes, and they fell right out the sky. They were the most comfortable clothes I ever owned." The man could tell a vivid story.

"Do you know what collards are?" I whisper to the nurse.

She looks at him. "No, but I know something he'll like," she says. The nurse escorts Blessed into the dayroom. Dr. Oberstein walks up.

"This is Blessed, he's from Alabama." The real names always come later.

"From the South again. They come in threes," says Dr. Oberstein.

"We have the phenomenon in the U.S. too," I say. When I did a rotation in the emergency room we would always see three heart attacks, three broken legs, etc. We became accustomed to looking for the third of any ailment.

Dr Oberstein takes a long examining look at me.

"Are you okay?" There is deep concern in his voice.

He's good. "A man grabbed me on the way here. The police tried to catch him but weren't able to."

"And your Israeli martial arts?" asks Dr. Oberstein, even more concerned.

"I broke his arm."

"Poetic justice," he assures with a slight satisfaction.

"But I didn't chase after him," I say almost with shame.

"Survival instinct. That's good, it's natural. You did the right thing." He always seems to have the right encouragement for me.

Dr. Oberstein takes the blood sample vial from my hand.

"Take the rest of the day off. We can send this sample out. I will see you here Sunday."

"Sunday?" I ask, confused.

"We work Sunday through Thursday."

•••

When I reach our street, I can see that Cohen is already in conversation with a Muslim neighbor. Both are holding a plate of food.

"Journey, this is Atiya. She lives on the next street over."

"Welcome," Atiya says.

Atiya hands me the dessert plate that she is holding.

"Thank you. That was very thoughtful of you." I smile.

Cohen translates what I said into Arabic.

"You're welcome," Atiya says, using the few English words she knows.

Cohen fills in the rest of the conversation that I must have missed, "It's called kanafeh. It is a very traditional Arabic dessert. You'll love it."

Atiya speaks in Arabic to Cohen, "Again, I am very sorry about my neighbor's little girl. She told me all about it. She cried all morning."

"Please tell her I forgive her," he replies in Arabic.

The woman nods, smiles, and walks away. Cohen pulls me to his chest and gives me the best hug possible while we are both still holding our desserts. He looks at me just as one tear falls down my face. He wipes it away with his thumb and kisses my cheek.

"I had a bad day," I confess.

"You want to sit on my balcony and talk about it?" His voice is tender.

"What are my other options?"

"I wanted to invite you to a wedding. Sorry for the late notice, but I got invited today." He shakes his head and says, "Construction workers," as if that explained the late invite.

"That sounds nice."

"Can you be ready in an hour? We will be eating there."

"Sure."

I return to my apartment, shower and dress. I choose to wear a simple tea-length teal dress. I stare in the mirror and wonder if the top of the dress is cut too low, and if it's too fitted. It's amazing how an aggressive act can make you question yourself. When I am convinced I am ready, there is a knock at the door.

I open the door to find Cohen, dressed in a light teal, short-sleeved shirt and white pants. I smile at the fact that we match.

"I do have a doorbell," I tease.

"I like to knock." He smiles back. He offers his arm, and I take it just after I grab my small purse and pull the door to lock.

"You look absolutely beautiful," he says.

"Thank you. You look very nice yourself. Thanks for matching."

"I tried," he says.

It is a short walk to the site of the wedding. I sit with Cohen on the groom's side, in an amazing ancient Jewish synagogue. I notice that Cameron and Tré are sitting together at the front of the synagogue, on the bride's side.

"Isn't that Cameron?" I whisper to Cohen.

Cohen doesn't answer. He just sits and takes hold of my hand. We stand and turn to watch the bride enter. My breath catches as the bride walks toward her groom, and the inexplicable *feeling* rushes over me again. We sit quietly through the beautiful ceremony. We watch as the groom breaks the glass. Soon the bride and groom walk out together. Tré makes eye contact with me and waves as if he is excited to see me.

At the reception, on a beautiful Jerusalem hotel rooftop, Cameron and Tré walk up to me and Cohen. Actually, Cameron goes right for Cohen. She kisses him and gives him a hug. "I didn't know you would be here," she says to him with a smile. She approaches me and gives me a kiss on the cheek. Her simple gesture seems infused with love and innocence. I feel my jealousy toward her soften. She smiles at me and radiates happiness.

She takes the inside of my arm and walks with me toward our dinner table. For a moment, I feel like an orphan she is tenderly guiding, and I enjoy the act of kindness. I have always intended to be a strong, independent woman. When I look at my life now, it seems I have surrounded myself with strong men. I am not sure whether this speaks for me or against me. Oblivious of my analytical thinking, she says "I didn't know that you knew Tré. He helps out at the orphanage. I asked him to come with me, from a month ago."

Tré gives me a kiss on the cheek, and we all sit down together. Cameron pulls her chair close to Cohen's. She puts her arm on his back to lean toward me and whispers, "I want you to know that I am not interested in Tré. He has been a good friend to me, and I asked him to come as a friend."

And then I understand why Cohen loves her so much. She immediately sensed my insecurities and addressed them. I smile at her and whisper back, "It's okay. I'm glad he is here."

Later, after dinner, we hear a Hebrew song that seems to start out like a prayer. Cohen looks at me, "Would you like to dance?" Some of the guests are doing assorted Israeli partner dances. I say yes, and he leads me to the dance floor. We begin to dance beautifully together. I took ballroom dancing in college, for fun, but never anything Israeli. But the way he led, it didn't matter. We dance a very close and graceful Israeli partner dance together.

"This is a beautiful song. What is she singing?" I ask Cohen as we dance.

"Don't Hate Me Because I Love You," he replies.

"For a wedding?" I ask.

"The DJ said that it is the bride's favorite song." We continue to dance and I get totally lost in the moment. He ends the dance with a dip.

"Let go," he says, my arms still around his neck. I release them gracefully down, feeling the strength of his hands holding me. I am mesmerized at how he knows, so very well, how to make me feel and look beautiful. He looks up, purposefully, from my gaze to somewhere or someone beyond me. He pulls me up with his strong arms. I feel the calluses on his hands through my dress.

"Thank you," Cohen says as he takes my hand and starts to walk me off of the dance floor. I look up to see that Cameron and Tré are heading toward the dance floor together. When we approach them, Cameron lets go of Tré's hand, as Cohen opens an arm to her. Cameron goes immediately to him, leaving Tré. Cohen still hasn't let go of my hand even though Cameron has made it very clear that his next dance is hers. There is an uncomfortable glance between Tré and Cohen before Cohen releases my hand. Tré puts his hands around my waist. It is clear that I am the one he wants to dance with. He walks me backward gently onto the dance floor. Cohen and Cameron dance simply together, her arms wrapped tightly around his neck, his arms around her waist; forehead to forehead, they whisper. Tré and I look at each other. Our dance is as simple; our chemistry is palpable.

Later, Cohen and Tré approach the bartender together. "Four glasses of red please," Tré requests in Hebrew.

"I'm sorry, but we are out of wine," the bartender replies.

"What?" Tré asks in unbelief.

"Everything they bought for the wedding, we put in that storeroom, and it's gone. I have already called the restaurant. It's closed, and no one in the building has the key," the bartender asserts himself in Hebrew.

82

Cohen asks politely, "You mind if I take a look?"

The bartender gestures toward the storeroom. "Bevakasha."

Cohen walks into the storeroom and comes out with a case of wine on his shoulder and places it behind the bar.

"I didn't see that," the bartender says, surprised. He continues in Hebrew to the other bartender, "Why didn't you see that?"

The second bartender just takes a bottle out of the box and begins uncorking it, "Box wasn't labeled."

The first bartender takes a bottle out and uncorks it as well, "Neither are the bottles." The bartender pours four glasses of wine. He hands the first two to Cohen who turns and hands them to Tré. Cohen takes the other two glasses and they start to make their way back to the table.

As they walk, Cohen looks over at Tré and says sincerely, "I'm sorry about your father."

Tré nods, a little surprised at his knowledge of this.

"You will have all of eternity to spend with him," Cohen adds with a comforting yet authoritative tone.

Tré's face softens, if only a little.

When they reach the table, Tré hands a glass to me and Cohen hands a glass to Cameron. Cohen is the first to raise his glass. "L'chaim."

"L'Chaim," we echo, toasting one another. When Cohen and Tré toast, Cohen looks at him as if he knew that something more than the toast has just transpired, and I can only presume that they are experiencing the rush of the *feeling* sweep over them, as it did me, when we were toasting together in Hebrew, "To life."

We have barely sipped from our glasses when the air raid sirens are sounded. The majority of guests run to clear the rooftop. I have no idea what's going on, and Tré grabs my hand and starts to pull me toward the exit. Cohen stands to catch the inside of my other arm.

"It's okay." Cohen says calmly.

"We're getting off the roof," Tré says assertively, defiantly.

Cohen pulls me close and whispers in my ear loud enough for me to hear, "You're with me," he says confidently. Needless to say, I felt torn.

Cameron, dutifully at Cohen's side, smiles as if Tré and I are acting ridiculous. Softly, confidently, she assures, "It's okay. You're with us."

It's not like I chose. I just couldn't move.

The first light from the Palestinian rocket lights up the sky, moving quickly but not as quickly as the other light moving like a shooting star to intercept it. My heart beats hard in my chest, and the sounds of the missiles resonate through my lungs.

"The Iron Dome." Someone actually said in English the words I had never heard used together before. I had no awareness of the security measure that I was witnessing.

Children stand with their mother as they look up at the lights like fireworks. If this mother allows her children to continue to witness this, how could we not be safe? "Echad," I hear the small boy say, and I realize he has started counting excitedly in Hebrew. I recognize the word for "one" in Hebrew from the "Shema" lesson.

I realize that Tré has stayed. He has positioned himself behind me. His arms are wrapped tightly around my waist. Cohen's hand is still encircling my upper arm. Cohen looks over at me and Tré as the lights are reflected in his pupils. It is a truly spectacular sight, and I am thankful to witness it. Thankful and sad. The boy counts out seven missiles fired at Jerusalem, and we watch as they are all successfully intercepted.

With the smell of sulfur still thick in the air, and the dance music that had never ceased, alive with life, "L'chaim," the festivities of celebrating a marriage resume.

All too soon, we all stand outside the hotel to exchange goodbyes. Tré's arm is around me. Cohen stands holding hands with Cameron and kisses her on the cheek. Cohen turns to Tré and says with authority, "I trust you will see Cameron home safely." He lets go of Cameron's hand, which is resistant to let go of his.

Tré hesitates for the briefest moment and replies, "I trust you with Journey." Tré gives me a quick kiss on the cheek, and releases my waist, yielding to Cohen's transportation arrangements, clearly defining the pecking order in Cohen's favor.

"But can I trust you?" Cohen's words are weighted.

There is silence among us all. Cameron breaks it. She kisses me on the cheek, "Good night," she says. She has the grace and beauty and timeless elegance of Grace Kelly. Except of course, when she is gazing at or admiring Cohen. Then she yields to her overwhelming love and shows no restraint in lavishing her affection on him.

Cohen extends his hand towards Tré. Tré accepts what he thinks is a goodbye handshake, and Cohen proceeds to pull him into a very masculine side hug. "Good night, Tré," Cohen says in Hebrew in an affirming, yet commanding tone.

That night I sleep in bed alone as the fan blows over me as well as the light breeze from the open balcony door. There is something very tranquil about this ancient city because, despite the heat, my sleep is so completely restful. I feel at home here, if only for this reason alone…I sleep well here. I lie completely comatose amidst this city, Jerusalem. *She* is a resounding testament to the love and a commitment of her Lord and God.

Chapter Six

The next day as I walk down a quiet street in Jerusalem, I hear a familiar voice. I look over to a park and see Melchizedek standing with a dozen or so followers seated at his feet. I walk up and stand on the outskirts of the group.

"The kingdom of heaven is like a treasure hidden in a field. When a man found it, he hid it again, and then in his joy went and sold all he had and bought that field." Melchizedek looks directly at me and asks, "Do you understand this?"

"No," I reply and wonder why he has to single me out.

"The treasure is salvation. When you understand the value of it; it is your joy to give up all that you have and are, to have it."

I take a deep breath.

"Do you want that treasure?"

"Yes." My answer surprises even me.

"Are you ready to buy the field?"

"No." I answer him honestly. The words have barely escaped my mouth when I see that Aki is approaching. "Go!" I urge Melchizedek. He calmly gets up with his followers and starts to walk away. I start to head in a different direction because I don't want to be involved.

Aki is amazingly fast and yells to me in English as he approaches, "Stay here." He continues to run toward Melchizedek. I decide to run in the opposite direction because I really don't want to get involved in this at all. Aki looks back at me and sees that I am running away. I am shocked when he changes direction and starts to pursue me instead of Melchizedek.

"Stop. I am Israeli security," he yells.

I instinctively run faster. I don't know him from Adam, and I am not about to get mixed up in something strange in a foreign country when I don't know who to trust. I feel my heart pounding. My mouth tastes like battery acid, and my head is beginning to ache with the rush of adrenaline. I continue to run even faster. I can hear that Aki is gaining on me. Why me?

He grabs my left arm. I turn back toward him as he pulls me. With momentum, I break out of his release with my left arm. I see and grab his gun from his pants with my right hand, as he reaches for it with his. I then take hold of his right arm with my freed left hand, twist it behind him, and force him to the ground with my knee in his back as I hold his own gun on him. This, in a fraction of a second.

Aki yells something in Hebrew and then realizes his mistake and yells the translation, "Get your hands off me, I am Israeli security." I can feel the sweat on his thick, dark arm hair but I have more than enough grip on him. When I don't respond he continues, "Remove your hands, I am Israeli security. My identification is in my back pocket."

I grab his badge from his pocket. How do I know it's real? I throw it on the ground in front of his face. My heart is in my throat, my hair is in my eyes, my muscles are aching, and I am really, really confused, afraid, and mad.

"Your identification means nothing to Israeli security. I saw you get arrested." I am surprised at how loudly and fiercely I am yelling.

"I just wanted to talk to you," he insists.

"If you're Israeli security, then call for backup."

His cell phone is on the ground near his face. Aki takes his free hand and throws his cell phone a good forty feet, but still in view. He fails my test.

"Give me my gun, and I will call for backup. If you don't cooperate with me, then I can't call for backup without you being arrested," he says quietly.

"No...or you will be arrested," I counter. I am surprised at how mean I can sound when I am being attacked." There is a deep quality in my yell that I have never heard in myself.

He attempts to maneuver out. I take the safety off the gun. I look around for someone, anyone, for help, to no avail.

"I am going to let go of you, but if you get up I *will* shoot you," I yell.

I lied. This was not a stalemate.

I back away from him and then run away. He gives me a ten-second start and then runs after me. He runs up and down the side streets. I can hear his feet running hard on the pavement, grunting as he breathes. I can only assume he is swearing intermittently. I try to quiet my breathing as I crouch behind the gate of an abandoned church, ironic for Jerusalem. I dare to view him for a millisecond. He is on the other side of the street. He spits the blood that he realizes is in his mouth. Then he wipes his lip, looking for the source of the bleeding area. I then hear him run back toward the park where he first spotted me and Melchizedek.

Much, much later, I am still crouched in the same place, still holding the gun, when I decide that it might be safe to leave. Finally I place the gun in my purse and walk quickly out of the gate, looking in both directions. I have barely gotten out of the gate when I see a forty-something Arab man. He walks up to various people who look like they don't understand what he is communicating, as he says nothing. I try to move away from him. I am afraid. I almost cower when he walks up. Still, he comes up to me with a flat expression on his face. He gets very close as I try to back away.

My fear segues to a medical curiosity. His pupils are unequal. I notice he is holding his arm, his right arm. I lift his sleeve, which reveals that his arm is obviously disfigured. I feel sorry for this man. An Arab woman is walking by. "Do you speak English?" I try to solicit her assistance.

"A little," she says.

"Ask him if he can speak," I request.

She asks him the question in Arabic, and he doesn't reply. I take out my cell phone and then think better of it. I walk him inside a small Jewish shop with antiques and jewelry. I help the man to a seat. The Arab woman is still at his side. The shop owner comes over to assist. "Do you speak English?"

"What's the problem?" He asks helpfully.

"Call for an ambulance. This man has had a stroke."

The store owner wastes no time in picking up the phone.

"Ask him if he wants to go to the hospital," I say to the Arab woman.

She asks him and he nods affirmatively. I check his pulse in both wrists as I tenderly work around the huge deformity on his right wrist. I use my hand to obscure the overhead light from his eyes to further assess his pupils, which are still unequal. The shop owner returns from the register area and says, "The paramedics are on their way."

I stay at the man's side although there is little that I can do for him, and it occurs to me that I recognize him. Before long we are outside and the paramedics are loading the Arab man onto the ambulance. I add my two cents, "Let the ER doctor know that he is having a stroke. He must have thrown a blood clot from his unrepaired arm."

"You just saw him fall?" They ask as they start to assess him.

"No. He didn't *just* fall. He broke his arm two days ago."

"You know this man?" the paramedic asks.

"No."

"How do you know he broke his arm?"

I pull up the man's sleeve. "His arm is disfigured, swollen, and the bruising is old." They turn towards the man as they hook him up to their equipment.

I finish my sentence under my breath, unheard. "And because I broke it."

The paramedics are about to close the doors. One of them looks back at me, "Are you coming?"

"No," I reply. He closes one door of the ambulance to reveal Aki coming towards me. Aki's affect is flat, but I sense that he is simmering below the surface. He is still on his hunt for me, but thankfully, he is looking the other way. I climb into the ambulance through the other open door. And we drive away.

When we reach the hospital, I stay at the Arab man's side. The ER doctor takes one look and says, "I think you're right. He is having a stroke. You may have saved his life. We will take good care of him, if you wouldn't mind waiting in the waiting room. It is through security, to your right."

Security means they search your purse. I can't be found with this gun. "The nearest exit?" I ask.

"Through security to your left," the doctor responds.

I move my purse from my side to my back as I bend down to tie my shoe and think. Just then another ambulance arrives and, as the paramedics rush in with another patient, I slip out the ambulance entrance.

As I climb onto Bus 14 to make my way back home, I see that there are two seats open, one by a religious man, the other by an Israeli police officer, wearing a holstered gun. I choose the seat next to the religious man. He gets up and walks away. I remain seated, holding my purse in my lap.

...

I sit on Cohen's couch as he examines the gun after I have recounted my busy afternoon. Cohen holds the gun flat in his hand as he looks at it. He shifts his focus from the gun to me as I look openly apprehensive about his verdict.

"It's Shin Bet: Israeli internal security," he says definitively.

"You think he is Shin Bet?" My anxieties heighten.

"He *is* Shin Bet," Cohen asserts.

"Maybe he stole their gun," I say refusing to believe that Aki would be a legitimate official.

"Not a chance."

"Why not? I did."

"Humanly unforeseeable circumstance," he asserts in Aki's defense.

"If he was Shin Bet, why didn't he call for backup?"

"You had his gun. In Israel this is very disgraceful," Cohen explains.

"What do I do? Should I take it in to them?" I offer, but believe me, it's the last thing I would want to do.

"No. Don't worry. I will take care of it," Cohen says. That is enough for me at the moment. I believe him.

I feel slightly relieved.

"That's not my only problem," I confess.

"You want to sit out on my balcony and talk about it?"

We sit out on his balcony and I tell him about the parable that Melchizedek shared. I look to him for his response.

"Journey," he begins, his voice is soft and filled with love and wisdom, "when that parable was first told, the field represented the world." He lets that statement sink in, then

91

continues, "And salvation is not something that you can earn…The treasure is you."

I look at him as I try to grasp his perspective.

"Journey, the treasure is you…Then who bought the field?"

"The Messiah." I give him the answer that I thought his question begged. It is not at all like I wholly believed it.

"Yes."

This time the *feeling* rushed over me not like a wave, but a series of waves challenging my very humanity…a series of warm, tingling sensations so powerful, so sweet, so utterly intoxicating to the heart that I thought if it continued—and with everything in me I wanted it to—it would end my physical life.

···

The next morning, I can hear Tré and Cohen talking in front of my apartment. Tré reaches my front steps at the same time as Cohen, who is looking very nicely dressed. Tré is breathing faster than the walk would warrant, and it didn't seem a good combination with the sight of Cohen.

"Shabbat Shalom," Cohen greets Tré.

"Shabbat Shalom."

Cohen and Tré always speak in Hebrew to one another. "Would you like to come to Shabbat service with me?" Cohen asks Tré.

Tré looks at Cohen and then at my front door. Then he turns back to Cohen.

"No, thank you."

"You've come to invite Journey to go with you?" Cohen's words are more a suggestion than a question.

"Yes."

Cohen looks at Tré until this is actually true.

"Good…Tré, I am going to see Cameron tomorrow at her new orphanage. I am going to dig a well for them."

"She will be relieved." Tré replies, possibly rejecting the invitation to join Cohen in helping out.

They part ways as Cohen walks off; Tré knocks on my door.

Tré holds true to the words he spoke to Cohen, and soon I am sitting in a Messianic Jewish synagogue, holding Tré's hand. We sing the Shema for my first time. The service is in Hebrew, so I don't get a lot out of it. I can't blame Tré: he speaks Hebrew, and this is his place of worship. I admire his bilingualism. I do my best to recite the liturgy even though I am sure if I knew what I was saying, I would probably be lying. The service is beautiful even though it makes me shamefully aware of my Western self-centeredness. Even the Spanish that I learned in grade school had been lost in brain synapses that have never again been fired.

I did enjoy my time at the service because as always, people of faith, while they shame me, intrigue me so. Perhaps, while sitting there, not yet knowing the language, I wondered, but even more now, where Cohen went to Shabbat service that day.

After Temple, Tré and I walk to Ben Yehuda Street to an outdoor café. We sit outside and have a falafel. There is a stir of people enjoying the food and music.

"This is amazing," I say, truly enjoying the culture. The freshly fried falafel has just enough spices in the ground chickpeas. It is generously garnished with a thin garlic-immersed tahini sauce, on a warm flatbread, complete with diced cucumbers and tomatoes. I take a moment to loathe my own country's dependence on fast food. I let my eyes wonder from Tré's handsomely sculpted face to a ten-year-old boy who plays the saxophone nearby. His instrument, a servant in a master's hands. I look at his kippah, centered meticulously in place. It makes me wonder if he struggled with whether it is lawful to play on the Shabbat or whether carrying his

93

instrument was considered work. I imagine the weight and toil of the Jewish law I could never live under. As taken as I am with his talented perfection, my eyes beg to return to their home, Tré. "Israel is amazing. I can see why you wanted to stay," I say.

"Why did you come to Israel?" Tré asks in a conversational tone.

His question feels more probing than, perhaps, he intended. I find myself referencing *Casablanca* once more, "For the water."

"There is no water in Israel. It's a desert," he replies, obviously understanding my reference.

"Well, I was misinformed," I reply continuing the charade.

"Friday, I will take you to the Dead Sea. I call it the Salt Sea. It is so bitter with minerals that it burns your tongue. There is Scripture that says that one day water will stream from the eastern side of the Temple and flow into the Salt Sea and make the waters fresh."

"That's a beautiful analogy."

"It's not just an analogy. It's a prophetic word…It will happen." Tré takes my hand and smiles. "Visualize it."

And I do try to visualize it, along with a sovereign master plan that is unfolding history through an ancient divinely inspired word. As I attempt this, it is truly difficult. My mind can only go back to the music as the musician's song ends. He begins another, the Shema, and I realize there is no lawful conflict in the boy's mind. I am the person with the conflicting laws and rules and distorted view of God, if He even exists. I can't even open a picture album or a medicine cabinet, for crying out loud. I almost get choked up.

"Wait, what's going on?" Tré is so sensitive. In Cohen's words, "he understands me."

I struggle to speak over the tightness in my throat, "I want to see your baby pictures," is all I can articulate for now.

He smiles and is amused at my untimely request, but I can tell he doesn't think I am crazy. "You can see my baby pictures. But I have to tell you that I was really ugly. Even my mom thought so."

I manage to laugh, and it is my salvation.

"My sister cried at the first look at me, really," he adds. Tré's ministering hand takes hold of mine, knowing my struggle is beyond my simple words. And I stop with all the thinking and just let the music and his hand be enough for now.

Before long, the beautiful, somewhat peaceful day has nearly ended, and I find myself on the steps of my apartment with Tré. In front of my door, he hugs me and gives me a goodnight kiss. I hand him my keys, and he opens the door. He hands the keys back to me. I look at him a little confused.

"Don't invite me in," he says.

"You're not coming in?" I am confused.

Tré smiles and then says in a joking manner, "Now that Cohen has a gun, he might shoot me. I'm surprised he's not waiting on your steps with it. He is very protective of you…and I'm okay with that."

"He doesn't need a gun to kill you," I joke back.

"Don't remind me." He changes the subject, "Tomorrow I plan to help Cohen with the well. You can come if you want."

"I have to work," I say apologetically.

"If your plans change, you should come."

He gives me a little kiss goodbye, as if anything more would make him go back on his decision to leave.

That night, in the stillness, after Tré had left, my eyes wandered toward the Bible that Elizabeth had given me. I hadn't thrown it out like chaff as I did the challah bread. It bothered me that everyone seemed to know more about this book than I did. Ignorance is not something I take kindly to. So I hesitantly picked up the Bible.

Reading someone else's Bible was more personal than I thought it would be. Elizabeth had highlighted and underlined various verses, and I have to say, for the most part, she chose the most interesting ones. The pages were worn, and some of them appeared to have gotten wet. There was faint lipstick residue in the shape of a kiss over one of the verses. This woman gave me a book she truly loved. I read to understand Tré, to understand Israel...to perhaps understand God...if that's even possible.

I read through intermittently where the highlights would take me. I also read through the beginning...creation...a theory I had long since abandoned. I read it through the context of the "appearance of age," and it was a little easier to consider. I read through the tireless genealogies which, although they were very dry—a list of consecutive names and ages—shed light on the biblical history of man. They suggested less fragile DNA, as exemplified by the long lifespans. What purpose did these genealogies serve?

I read through some of the detailed books of the law. They exhausted me. They haunted me.

I read through some of the psalms. Man, were they worn and marked. Elizabeth had really worn out some writing utensils on them. I could understand why...I near about fell in love with David.

I read through some of the red-letter chapters and some of the study guides at the bottom of the pages that reference Old Testament Scripture. I was in awe of the research that had

96

been done. The genealogies were in the red chapters also. Was this controversial historical figure related to the passionate psalm writer? According to the Bible, it seemed so. I read with, and at times without, a piety that favored science. I read with, and at times without, a fascinated curiosity. I always read with an eye for the poetic…a lifted eyebrow to the violence and the depravity of man. The fall, the rise, the forgiveness. I read until I was sleepy.

Then the gentle breeze from my open balcony door, and the sounds of the restless city, wooed me to sleep.

They say that the best way to study something is to read it before you sleep. And I wondered, when my body rested, whether my mind did, too, or if it pondered through the ancient words? Were they really alive and active…sharper than a double-edged sword, penetrating even to dividing soul and spirit, joints and marrow; judging the thoughts and the attitude of the heart? Elizabeth apparently thought so. I, on the other hand, wasn't sure.

•••

The next morning, I am sitting in the living room when my phone rings.

"Hello?"

"Journey, hello, this is Yonathan. Dr. Oberstein wanted me to call you and tell you that we don't have any new admits if you want the day off."

"Yes. Thank you." So as Tré hoped, I had the day off after all.

•••

Cohen, Tré, and I are seated on the bus to Northern Israel. I keep casually looking back at a young Israeli soldier, not more than eighteen years old. He has closed his eyes. The trigger of his large rifle is resting between his legs, and the barrel of it is cradled in his arms. Youth and innocence,

97

clothed in duty, strength, and war. I feel both grateful and sad for him at the same time.

···

Unbeknownst to me, at about that same time, Aki was in a Shin Bet forensics gun laboratory. A gun in a plastic bag is placed on the intake table between Aki and the forensic researcher.

"Tell me everything about this gun," Aki states.

The researcher looks at it for the briefest second and then types the serial number in the computer.

"It's your gun, you tell me," the researcher states.

"It's not my gun," Aki insists.

"It's registered to you," the researcher challenges.

"It's not my gun. Tell me everything about it."

"I'll call you," the forensic researcher replies, less than thrilled.

···

Tré, Cohen, and I stand looking at the orphanage. It leaves a lot to be desired. The dilapidated building stands on a large piece of dry land.

"It's nice," I say politely as I cut my eyes over to Tré. I give him a look that contradicts my words. Cohen looks at the orphanage and smiles, pleased. We walk up to the door and knock. When Cameron opens the door, she has a baby on her hip and a toddler hugging her leg.

"You're here!" Cameron hugs Cohen and kisses his face until it's almost uncomfortable. The baby immediately goes to Cohen and hugs him. Cohen gives him a kiss. He reaches down and picks up the toddler. "This is Sarah," Cameron says as she touches the toddler's head and looks toward us. "And this is Rivka," Cameron gestures to the young orphanage worker. Sarah goes willingly into Cohen's arms without hesitation. She smiles at him, and he kisses her. Cameron kisses me, then Tré. We introduce ourselves to Rivka and the children.

Cameron musters some enthusiasm, "So this is it. It's great. Did you see the land out there?" So we *all* ignore the elephant in the room that is her seemingly wretched new orphanage.

"Yes, it's beautiful," I say, still appalled at the depravity of the place.

Cameron takes a wipe and wipes Sarah's face. "They're so dirty. I'm sorry. They're never like this," she says. She starts to cry. Cohen hands the baby to Rivka and puts Sarah down. He walks over to Cameron and takes her face in his hands. He wipes her tears and looks her squarely in the eyes. "It's temporary," he says comfortingly.

"You're going to have a well today," Tré assures her.

"All of this is temporary," Cohen whispers to Cameron. He takes her hand and leads her outside, leaving the front door open. He walks her out about forty feet and stands behind her with his arms around her.

Still inside, I kneel down to Sarah.

"Shalom." I try to win her over with the little Hebrew that I know. She runs and hides behind Rivka's legs.

Rivka says, "She's shy."

Tré takes out his camera to start a conversation with a five-year-old boy. "What's your name?" Tré asks in Hebrew.

"Caleb," the boy says.

"This is my camera. Do you want to see it?" Tré asks.

"Can I take a picture?" Caleb asks.

Tré holds the camera and demonstrates how to take a picture. "Point at what you want to take a picture of and just push this button," Tré says in Hebrew, and I understand through his actions. As Tré explains this, he takes a picture of Cameron and Cohen as if he couldn't resist the composition. He looks at Rivka to see her thoughts on his action.

"Oh, Cameron will love that picture," she assures him.

99

Caleb speaks up to correct Rivka for calling Cameron by her name. "Emma," he insists. Tré hands the camera to Caleb, who takes a picture of Sarah.

Rivka explains Caleb's remark, "They all call her 'Emma,' Momma. We don't teach them that. They just all do it."

I smile at the thought of the children looking to her as a mother. I look over at her and Cohen in the distance, marveling at their relationship. I try to hold back this covetous feeling that I have for what they have together. I make an effort not to stare, looking to the children and to Tré.

Before long Cohen and Cameron come back through the door, still holding hands. Cohen motions for Tré to go work. Cameron is smiling, her face almost glowing.

"What did he say to you?" I ask curiously.

"All the right things," she replies.

Cameron is more than smiling. She has a twinkle in her eye. I am completely intrigued. She apologizes for her ambiguity, "There's no translation."

...

At the site of the well, Cohen and Tré are dirty. They are at work with some elaborate equipment, and have made progress with the well. Tré says, "You're not tired?"

Cohen replies, "It's okay if you take a break. Just don't give up on me. If you're committed to something; be committed to it."

Tré asks, "Are you talking about Journey, or God?"

"Both. You have the same problem with both. You're not committed."

Tré responds, "That's not true."

Cohen stops for a moment and looks Tré square in the eyes. "I'm lying?" Cohen pauses for a moment and continues, "You could be standing under a rainbow with a ring in your pocket and the perfect woman in front of you...and you would still be afraid to commit."

100

Tré musters a denial, "I wouldn't be afraid."

Cohen looks at him until Tré's words are true.

"Good," Cohen says abruptly. Then he opens his arms to Tré and they hug.

I can see them from the orphanage doorway. I stand with a cleaning cloth in my hand and look to see what all the commotion is about. I say to Cameron, "I don't know what it is, but since I've been in Israel, I've seen people arguing in Hebrew, like they are so mad at each other they are about to fight; and then all of a sudden they are smiling and hugging each other."

Without hesitation she replies, "We're passionate people."

Sarah pulls at my clothes; finally ready to make friends. Sarah speaks in Hebrew, not realizing that I can't understand a word she says. Cameron translates, "She says her room is going to be pink and purple." Then she clarifies Sarah's statement with her in Hebrew, "Do you want your room to be pink or purple?" Sarah assertively echoes some of the same Hebrew words back to Cameron and Cameron then translates again to me. "'Pink *and* purple, with butterflies and flowers' and we have no money for paint. I don't even know how we are going to afford this place." Cameron smiles anyway and says, "This is my life."

●●●

It is almost dark when Cohen stops working on the well. "It's almost finished. You will need to leave, if you're going to make the bus back to Jerusalem."

Tré references their earlier conversation, "I'm committed to finishing this well."

Cohen says assertively, "I'm asking you to take Journey home safely. I'm going to need to say goodbye to Cameron."

"How will you get home?" Tré asks.

Cohen points his index finger down to the ground, the Israeli hitchhiking gesture.

• • •

Tré and I make the commute home without Cohen. As we reach my doorway, he begins to kiss me goodnight, and it takes a passionate turn. In seconds, I am against the door, both of us breathless. We pull away at the exact same second, and we both look as though we surprised each other by this, as though it were the last thing we would've thought possible from each other.

Tré clears his throat and tries to regain composure, "Were you going to say something?"

I try to muster a response, "I was…I want to say goodnight." I try to explain further, "When you stay…your conversation isn't as deep…and I really feel like I need that right now. What were you going to say?"

Tré says, "I was going to say goodnight."

He opens my door and hands my keys to me. I accept my keys with one hand as I place my other hand firmly on his chest. It is there for restraint if need be as I say, "I wouldn't have really been able to stop, if you hadn't." My words are clearly a confession, not an invitation.

Tré also confesses, "I wouldn't have really been able to if you hadn't either." I can tell that he understands my context.

"Thank you," I say, referring to the fact that *we* have been able to stop.

He replies, "Thank you."

I close the door as he turns away. I still don't like the sight of him walking away from me.

• • •

The next morning, Cohen is out in front of where he lives. He is obviously mixing mortar with water. Stones are in a pile, in the front of the house.

"So does Cameron have water?" I ask.

"The well is finished. I told her to let it set for three days."

"That makes sense. Things probably have to settle," I say. "What are you doing?"

"I am restoring this to its original architecture for the homeowner."

"You don't have to go to work today?" I ask.

"No, I am working on this for the next few days." He looks up at me and smiles, squinting through the sun. "Would you hand me one of those?" he asks, pointing to the pile of stones.

I pick up a stone. I look at it but I see another stone that looks shinier. I put the first one down and reach for the shiny stone and hand it to Cohen.

"Thank you," he says as he accepts the stone and places it down at his side. "Would you hand me that one, also?" He gestures to the first stone I picked up. I give it to him. He places this stone on the corner of the house and starts the restoration.

"Those stones are so smooth. I wonder how old they are?" I ask, just making conversation.

"They were just made." Cohen replies.

"They're synthetic? You're kidding…They look ancient," I say.

"Things aren't always what they seem," Cohen says.

"I have to go to work," I say, as I walk up behind where he is kneeling. I give him a kiss on the cheek. He turns toward me and does the same.

"And find Melchizedek?" he asks.

"And find Melchizedek," I say affirmatively as I walk away.

Chapter Seven

At the hospital, I check my work area to see if there are any samples to observe. Dr. Oberstein appears in the doorway of the lab and says, "Shalom, Journey. There are no new admits. Can I please see you for a moment in my office?"

I sit at the other end of Dr. Oberstein's desk. I try to nonchalantly brace myself mentally for what he could possibly have to speak so formally with me about.

"How was your weekend?" he asks.

"Fine." I manage to smile.

"Any sign of Melchizedek?" he asks, almost conversationally.

"No," I lie.

"No sign of Melchizedek?" he asks again, with the slightest bit of accusation.

"No. I did not see him," I say, trying to look into eyes that are usually filled with warmth but are now stone-cold. He looks disappointed with the way that I have answered.

"Journey," he says, "I called you in here because I had a visit from Shin Bet a few moments ago. The same man called last week just after the appearance of Melchizedek, which contributed to my interest in him. We often work with Israeli police when they apprehend patients who are indecent or out of control. We have never worked with *Shin Bet*. Today, the officer was looking not only for information about Melchizedek, but also about an American girl who fit your physical description. But the girl he mentioned, he said, was aggressive…and I knew that that could not be anyone that I know."

I could tell that his words were contrasting his thoughts. They hung between us for an uncomfortable moment while I tried to think.

"You told him this?" I finally manage to respond.

"Yes…but I feel that it is important for us to work with Shin Bet. They are there for our protection." Dr. Oberstein hands me a business card with a telephone number on it. The officer's name, Aki Reznikoff, is printed in English. So this is who has been chasing me. Apparently closing in on me, to give a card in English. A similar card in Hebrew is on the corner of Dr. Oberstein's desk. Dr. Oberstein walks over to look through the blinds as he continues his conversation with me. "Israeli security can be very intimidating. You have been through a lot in the last week. I would like you to call this man and talk…about Melchizedek…when you are ready. Perhaps you should take the day off; no, as much time as you need to take care of this."

"Thank you," I say, clearly understanding his polite ultimatum. I stand and walk toward the door. Dr. Oberstein continues to look out the blinds.

"And Journey," Dr Oberstein says, his voice as even as before.

"Yes?"

"Have you seen the garden at the back of our hospital?"

"No."

"You should see it. Why don't you walk out that way?"

"Thank you," I say sincerely, understanding from Dr. Oberstein's words and actions that the Shin Bet officer is out front waiting for me.

Had I not walked out the back and continued on another route, I would've seen Aki standing in front of the hospital.

Aki paces back and forth in front of the hospital. His phone rings and he answers in Hebrew. "This is Aki," he says abruptly.

The forensic researcher on the other end says, "You are right…it's not your gun."

"Exactly. How did you know?" Aki says, gratified by the findings.

The forensic researcher continues on the other end of the phone, "The gun has never been fired. Both the gun and the bullets are virtually untraceable, except the prints, which also come up empty."

"One set of prints?" Aki asks for clarification.

"Yes."

"Male or female?"

"They suggest male." The researcher answers in careful terms, as they always do.

I sit with my sunglasses on, riding the Jerusalem Bus 14 home. Elizabeth boards the bus and sits beside me.

"Hi. I remember you," she says.

"Yes. Hi, how are you?" I reply.

"Good."

"Have you seen Melchizedek lately?" I inquire.

"Yes," Elizabeth says, "And I'm planning to meet him on Wednesday at the park near the cinematheque…if you want to come."

"I would like to come," I say excitedly. "Do you believe he is who he says he is?"

"Yes, I do. I have a little issue with the way that he told the parable of the treasure, and that is what I am meeting him to talk about."

"I'm having an issue with that, too," I say, surprised at the coincidence.

"Oh, well, then it will be good if you come. What about you? Do you believe he is who he says he is?" she asks back.

"I like the idea of the possibility that I have seen God face to face. I don't know if I believe, but I'm not sure if I'm quite ready to let go of that possibility either," I confide to her.

The bus stops at my stop. "I'll see you on Wednesday," I say as I exit the bus. She smiles and waves.

...

When I approach Cohen, he is finishing the front of the house. When I first see it, I have to stop walking and stand to marvel at it. It is truly remarkable how much progress he has made. It's almost unbelievable.

"Cohen, it's amazing," I say.

He looks back at me and smiles.

I am bursting at the seams to get some insight into Dr. Oberstein's revelation. "I'm having another problem," I say to him, and soon, as has become our custom, I find myself standing on his balcony. I recount my conversation with Dr. Oberstein. I realize that I am pacing back and forth on his balcony. Cohen gestures for me to sit. I feel too worried to sit.

"Sit. Don't worry," he says.

"Should I call him?" I sit down and hold onto the arm rests for strength.

"Call him when you're ready."

"What about the gun?"

"Taken care of," he responds.

"If I don't call him, do you think that he will find me?"

"He's Shin Bet. He will find you. And when he does—you can trust him."

Just then my phone rings and I nearly fall out of the chair. I answer the phone. "Tré, hi, how are you?"

He asks if I got the day off, and soon I am floating in the Salt Sea with him.

•••

The viscous water only reaches our shoulders because of our buoyancy. The sun shines down on us as I admire Tré through my rose-colored aviator sunglasses. "This is medicinal," I say.

"It's funny you should say that, because physicians actually prescribe time in the Salt Sea for skin conditions like eczema and psoriasis."

"Really? You're so knowledgeable."

We give each other a little kiss. I lick my lips, smile, and shake my head like I've just taken a shot of hard liquor. I wince at the bitter flavor of the water.

We lie on the beach together. He rubs my arm to show me that small crystals have formed on my arm where the water has evaporated. Then he points to some people along the shore, who have covered their arms and legs with the mud.

"This is great," I say, enjoying being a tourist, while forgetting I am practically a fugitive. We give each other a small, truthful kiss.

"Tré?" I start off, feeling that the truthfulness of the moment should continue.

"Yes."

"I didn't come here for the water…I didn't come here for the fellowship at the hospital, and I didn't come here just for you," I confess.

"People come to Israel because they are searching for something…Have you found what you are looking for?" he asks.

"No…but I think I can almost visualize it. What about you? Have you found what you were looking for?"

"Yes," he says without hesitation, "And then some."

On the bus ride home, I can't help taking notice through the window that the sky is a shade somewhere between pink and purple. Subliminally, I think of Cameron's unrelenting heart to provide for the wants and needs of the orphans she has been entrusted with. I undoubtedly know that Sarah will get her pink and purple room, complete with the butterflies and flowers.

When we reach my apartment, Tré opens the door. There is a kiss goodbye. He hands me the keys with no conflict, but looks as if he had something more to say.

"What is this look?" I can't help but ask.

"I'm just content."

"Me, too."

The next day I go to the Tel Aviv beach by myself just to think, and perhaps to hide. I search for answers as the waves roll in.

Later that night, I spar with Cohen in his living room. We spar until I am completely exhausted. Cohen has me in a hold on the floor. We stop fighting at the exact same moment. I close my eyes and just lie in his arms and let the *feeling* sweep over me. I lie in his arms completely comfortable except for a strand of hair over my eye. It's bothering me, but I choose not to move. I think if I move, it will initiate him to move, and I want to stay here with him just as we are. Just then, Cohen reaches up and removes the hair from my eye. He then resumes the position we had been in.

"That was bothering me," he says.

I lie there with him a truly unknown length of time. It's as if time had somehow lost its meaning, and I didn't have a care in the world. Eventually, without a word, I move to leave, he helps me up, and I head home.

The next day I tour the garden tomb. I stare at a sign that reads, "He is not here, for he is risen."

When I return to our street, I can only stare in disbelief at the progress that Cohen has made on the house. As he guides me, I walk completely around the house to see that the restoration is complete. He then ushers me into the house. "I can't believe it's finished," I keep repeating. Cohen nods and smiles. He looks sad...ill...worried?

"Journey, I went by the hotel today. It's completed. Soon I will be moving on to other work. You must continue to seek and share the truth. Despite any setbacks or times when you may feel faithless...you must believe that you have a purpose."

I look at his neck to see petechiae...little bruises...like broken capillaries forming quickly on his neck, then down to his chest. Droplets of blood form slowly through the profuse tiny purple dots like perspiration beads. He is bleeding spontaneously out of his pores. I can't believe my eyes. I open his shirt, to see that blood is slowly emerging there also. "I'm calling for an ambulance. You might have a bleeding disorder...your platelets must be low," I say. Cohen takes hold of my arm, in defiance.

"I don't need to go to a hospital," he says.

"I can't help you here," I insist. He continues to hold my arm, conveying that he is in control.

"Cohen, please, I can't sit here and watch you bleed to death," I plead. I look through the glass balcony doors searching for a solution. I notice that it is starting to turn dusk, and I remember that it is Wednesday. "Can I take you to Melchizedek?"

"Do you believe that a touch from a priest in the order of Melchizedek can heal?" he asks.

"Yes," I say, desperate to try anything.

"Then I will go with you."

It is a short walk to the Jerusalem park. We walk arm in arm, and I am utterly surprised that he isn't putting more weight on me. I can see that Melchizedek stands in the park alone. Cohen's blood is now all over my shirt and face. I am completely out of breath, as Cohen and Melchizedek come face to face.

"Do you believe that a touch can heal?" Cohen asks him.

"Yes," replies Melchizedek. Cohen reaches out his hand and they grasp hands for a moment.

Melchizedek falls to his knees, in shock, realization…worship?

"You are the treasure," Cohen says lovingly but with authority.

I fall to my knees also to either attend to Melchizedek or get his attention. Cohen, still bleeding, walks over the hill and away from us.

"He is everything I thought I was. He is the man who bought the field…the true priest in the order of Melchizedek," says Melchizedek, as I knew him.

It is one of those moments when you see something happen and you somehow realize that you should understand it, but you don't. Or you do, but it has to sink in. It's as if you are trapped in the surreal. I am so confused. I get up and walk over the hill to look for Cohen. He is nowhere to be found. I run frantically throughout the park, desperately looking for him. If what Melchizedek, or whoever just bowed to Cohen, said is true…then Cohen is the elusive character…this God incarnate. My knees crumble beneath me there at the corner of the park. I am forced to sit on the dusty stone sidewalk and try to catch my breath, unable to move, just barely able to think. Still. Thoughts seem more like my enemies now. This couldn't possibly make sense.

Memories. Memories feel more like friends. I cling to them, as memories of Cohen flood my mind. I want to shake my head at the lunacy that this truth somehow managed to remain hidden. The epiphany unfolds as Cohen's words flood back to me, "If you were standing face to face with God, would you recognize him?" He provided wine at the wedding. He sparred with me, wrestling like the proverbial "angel" who left Jacob saying, "I have seen the face of God and lived." He asked me for the cornerstone that I rejected. He restored the building in three days. He provided a home for the orphans and a new home for the widow. True religion. He wrestled with *me*. I bask in the realization of who he is as it wars with my intellect. A Christophany.

He was the omnipresent, unchanging stimulus that disappears, as defined by Troxler's fading. My focal point had been my career, then Tré, and quite possibly the Melchizedek, as I previously knew him. And now that I directed my vision from my previous focal points, I could clearly see Him. I could see and know that He had always been there.

Chapter Eight

It was about the same time at the orphanage in Northern Israel when Cameron walked out to test the well. The sun is giving off golden light the way that it does just before dusk.

Zach, a ten-year-old boy who lives at the orphanage, runs out to join Cameron. Both he and she have buckets in their hands.

"It's been exactly three days. Let's get some water," Cameron says excitedly. She tries to extract water from the well and thick black liquid comes out.

"What?" she exclaims, very disappointed.

Zach smiles and interprets the situation much differently. "Emma! I think we've struck oil!" he says enthusiastically.

...

And it was about that same time, when Tré was in a darkroom developing the pictures he had taken from the day that we went to the orphanage. Tré watches as the picture of Cameron and Cohen develops. The doorway of the orphanage, in the picture, frames Cameron and Cohen beautifully, but it is an obvious challenge to expose the whole picture properly. The sky appears "blown out" in this first picture. He attempts another. He uses his hands to "dodge and burn" the light. His eyes examine the picture very carefully as the image starts to appear more clear.

...

I knock on Cohen's door, and when there is no answer, I find that the door is unlocked. I walk throughout the house calling and looking for him. The last place I look for him is in the bedroom, to no avail. In his bedroom I find that there are no clothes at all in the closet, no suitcase, no sign of him. To my dismay, however, on the dresser is Aki's gun. I pick it up and walk out.

I walk into my house feeling disillusioned. I make my way to the bathroom mirror and stare into it, searching myself. Cohen's blood is still on me, evidence of an enigma I can't wrap my mind around. I want to walk into Kfar Shaul Hospital and look at his blood. I want to compare it to the DNA strands of tooth enamel that they found on the Shroud of Turin. I am struggling with the fact that I still want proof. How could this be faith? I wash the blood completely off of my face. I start to take off my bloody shirt. I throw wood in the fireplace and start a fire. I hold my shirt, with Cohen's blood on it, close to my chest. I smell it. I need to end this struggle in me. I accept that he found me, chose…me. And I accept him at his word, for who he is, through his blood…by faith and nothing more. The waves of the *feeling* rush over me, just as strong and as powerful as ever. I throw my shirt into the fire.

And with the final embers came regret, for everyone who needed or wanted what this evidence could have given them.

A short time later, I hear a knock at the door. I look out to see Tré and open the door. I know that it is more than evident that I have been crying. Tré enfolds me in a comforting embrace.

"What's wrong?" he says, concerned. "I've never seen you like this."

"Cohen started bleeding spontaneously out of his pores, and he wouldn't go to the hospital. So I took him to Melchizedek and Melchizedek said that Cohen was the true priest in the order of Melchizedek. And then Cohen walked away suddenly… and he was….gone. He's gone." I sob unashamedly to him. I pull on his clothes in grief.

Tré looks at me in disbelief, then realization. "He was bleeding…Blood was just coming out of him?" he asks.

"Yes."

"There were so many signs. I thought that God was talking to me through him…but I was talking to God—face to face."

"Then you believe it, too," I say as I look to him for affirmation.

Tré pulls a picture out of an envelope that I realize that he has with him. He shows the photo to me to reveal a remarkably distinct, obvious, face in the clouds above Cameron and Cohen.

"Yes," he answers after presenting the remarkable picture. I start to cry again.

"I'm going to miss him….his physical presence…so much," I say.

"We have all of eternity to spend with him," Tré says, echoing the words of comfort that Cohen previously offered him.

"There's something else," I confess.

"What?"

"I had Cohen's blood all over me, and it scared me when I thought about what I could do with it…what I might find or not find. I burned it…it's gone…Are you mad at me?"

"No. I think it was a beautiful sacrifice. And when I say that, I don't mean that it redeemed you…it showed your redemption." His words were soft and assuring.

"That's how it felt."

•••

I wake up the next morning to the usual stray cats. I walk over to Cohen's place and try to walk in. This time, however, the door is locked. I knock on the door. An older woman opens the door.

115

"Who are you?" I say, astonished to find someone else.

"I'm Michal. I live here. Who are you?"

"I'm Journey. I'm your neighbor."

She invites me in for a cup of tea. I share with her some of what has been going on, and I try desperately hard not to sound too crazy. Michal is still looking amazed when she says, "You can look around. But there is absolutely no trace of him here except the beautiful restorations I have always wanted."

She was right, there was no trace of him, and believe me, I looked. And as a scientist, I checked everything including the shower drain, for residual hair. I was looking for one shred of genetic evidence.

•••

It is on this morning that Aki's wife hands him the morning paper at the breakfast table. The paper has a huge picture of Cameron on the front of it. "Did you see the news? We have oil in Israel," she says.

Aki looks at the paper in disbelief. Then he picks up his cell phone.

•••

It didn't take long for Aki to find Cameron. He caught up with her at the Jerusalem hotel that Cohen had worked on.

Aki walks up to her. "Shalom," he says.

Cameron smiles and touches his face. He smiles. "Shalom," she responds.

•••

It is later, when I stand in a quiet Jerusalem park, that I get brave enough to take my cell phone out of my purse, as well as the gun and the business card. I summon up what is left of my bravery and dial the number. The phone rings.

"Hello, Journey," says Aki. I hear the voice on the phone in stereo and realize that he is right behind me. I am startled. I drop the phone and turn. It is this moment that I realize that I have his gun pointed directly at him yet again. Needless to say, we spar intensely.

This is not what I intended. I fought with him initially because I was just startled. I thought I had just a few more minutes to prepare.

And then I realize, somewhere in the act of moving faster than thinking, that I am fighting to remember what it was like with Cohen. The *feeling* sweeps over me, and perhaps Aki. I find myself in a hold that I can get out of but don't. He holds me there almost comfortingly until we both catch our breath. He stands behind me, his arms wrapped around me, holding the wrists of my crossed arms to each of my hips. With every breath, his cheek moves ever so slightly against mine. The five o'clock shadow of his thick, dark beard feels abrasive against my sensitive skin. Thinking through the vast chain of events, I hardly notice the enticing smell of his expensive, probably Italian cologne. The virile hunter and his beloved prey. For a moment, we are one.

"Cameron said you would come willingly," Aki says without the slightest bit of exaggeration.

"I'm sorry, I really just wanted to talk to you," I apologize.

He lets go of me and we walk to his car, as if what has just taken place was the equivalent of his showing me his ID and my consenting to go in for questioning.

Chapter Nine

When we arrive at Shin Bet headquarters, Aki escorts me into a room that is completely bare except for a table, two chairs, and a video monitor that is set on a stand.

"Where's Cameron?" I ask with authority.

"She's in another room. She's comfortable. Tré will be here soon, and I plan to question him. Now, if you don't mind, I have some questions for you. You visited the Wailing Wall the evening that…the prayers fell. Did you put a prayer in the Wall?" His crew-cut dark hair is now in perfect order. His eyes are the deepest turquoise as they stare into mine, awaiting my response. For the briefest moment, I admire them, and him.

"Yes," I reply.

"What did it say?"

"What?" I ask, confused at his line of questioning.

"The prayer, you put in the Wall—what did it say?"

I am clearly annoyed that he would have the nerve to ask. I can only figure it is some sort of interrogation technique, so I answer: "God, if you exist, please show yourself to me."

Aki takes a deep breath, as if I have given him something he was desperately waiting for. And this confuses me even further. I wonder what this is all about. He asks me about every moment with Cohen; every word of every conversation that I had or knew of. I answer every question, and I lie about nothing. He leaves the room intermittently for long periods of time, apparently questioning Cameron and Tré.

The last time he leaves the room, he is gone for quite a long time. When he reenters the room, he says, "You've answered all of my questions. You are free to leave."

I just sit there.

"What's wrong? Most people are glad when the interrogation is over. Ah. I suspect *you* have some questions for me," he says knowingly.

I start to reply, "I do…"

"Shh. I will make you a deal. I will answer your questions, if you agree to do a favor for Shin Bet." He says this in a quiet, bargaining tone.

"What is it?" I ask, trying to hide my interest.

"I cannot tell you unless you agree. I don't need *you* for the favor, I'm sure there are hundreds of other people who could do it. I want *you* to do it." He was almost smug.

Normally I would decline due to his cockiness alone, but I pause and remember Cohen's words.

"I trust you. I agree," I say.

"Then we have a deal." He seems pleased with my response.

"Yes. How…?"

He silences me by putting his index finger over his lips.

"Let me guess your questions," he says. Oh, this is fun for him. "You want to know how *I* knew about Cohen." At first I think he is being insolent…toying with me.

"Yes," I reply, willing to play, too, if I have to.

Aki walks over to the monitor and presses PLAY to reveal surveillance video of the Wailing Wall, from the evening the prayers fell. He points to a man whose back is to the camera, I start to assume the figure is Aki, from his stature. Cohen walks by and pats him on the back. Prayers are circling everywhere; one falls in front of Aki as security is escorting him out, a scene I am familiar with, only from a different angle. Aki pushes another button on the video player, and I see that Aki is seated, apparently being interrogated by an Israeli security officer who has an ID badge in his hand. From this angle, I am unable to make out the picture on the badge. The two are in a heated argument in Hebrew. Aki translates the images I see, with every bit of feeling:

"Let me ask you again. Where did you get this?" asks the security officer.

"And I will give you the same answer…it's mine," Aki replies.

The security officer says, "I just have one problem with that." The officer moves until he is face to face with Aki and yells, "It looks nothing like you!"

"Are you blind?" Aki asks the interrogator. "Call Shin Bet, I will give you their number."

The officer replies, "They are coming and so is your 'wife.'" The officer uses his fingers to denote quotation marks around that word, "wife."

Just then, Aki looks over at the two-way mirror. He runs toward the mirror and touches his face. "Oh, my God, my face is healed!" Aki's voice is filled with emotion. He moves his face closer to the mirror, wanting to believe. He moves his face back and forth in front of the mirror, as if he didn't believe it could possibly *be* a mirror.

The security officer rolls his eyes and holds up a piece of paper and walks over to Aki. He asks, "What is this? A joke? Is this your prayer that's been answered?" He hands Aki the piece of paper that he obviously has previously taken from him. Aki reads it almost presumptuously, "'Heal me'… Yes, I wrote this ten years ago and placed it in the Wall."

Just then the door opens, and Aki's wife walks in and then runs toward Aki.

"Aki!" In that one word she removes any further doubt. She touches his face. They hug and kiss and weep.

...

I am still sitting in the interrogation room, on the edge of my seat, when Aki stops the video player and places the ID badge in my hands. I stare at the photo on it, of a man with extensive facial burn scars, the bone structure and eyes undeniably Aki's. I put my hand over my mouth in disbelief.

Aki explains as I look back and forth from the picture to him. "They thought it was a case of identity theft or a fake ID."

My heart fills with compassion, and I dare to ask, "What happened to you?"

"Helicopter crash. I don't remember it at all," Aki says.

"And you were still Shin Bet with these scars?"

Aki smiles, "I'm good at what I do…they bent the rules for me."

Aki pushes PLAY on the monitor again. "Now watch you." He points to the monitor, describing the events as they unfold. "You put your prayer in the Wall. Cohen steps onto the platform. Watch your prayer. It comes out of the Wall, is caught in the wind, Cohen holds out his hand and catches your prayer, just after he's handed me mine." Aki rewinds.

"That's why you were looking for me," I say, finally making sense of the mystery.

Aki presses PLAY, then says, "Yes, now watch Cameron. She is walking toward the Wall. She sees Cohen touch me. She's the *only one* who sees him heal me. She stops walking toward the Wall and starts walking toward Cohen. And did you see that? She hands him her prayer, and he accepts it." I see it on the monitor just as he has narrated it, as subtle as it was.

"She knew!" I say, as the realization hits me.

"She's the only one who knew and still saw him afterward."

"Why didn't she say anything?" I ask, more rhetorically than seriously.

Aki answers anyway, "She said that as long as Cohen was around, she felt that that moment of realization belonged between the person and him." I shake my head trying to believe. Aki walks up to whisper in my ear. "And just to let you know, the day you stole my gun…When I got home, my wife told me I had left my gun on the table that morning." He backs away and adds, "The gun had my serial number and had never been fired."

"I wondered about that. He said he would take care of it," I reply.

"I wish the theologians and rabbis could contemplate *that* creation. But that's our secret…right?"

"Absolutely," I now considered myself his comrade, his friend.

"I have one more question for you." Either his questions are less threatening or I am just completely comfortable with him now.

"Yes?" I answer trustingly, almost hopeful for his next one.

"Why would God reveal himself to a geneticist?"

"I told you… I thought about comparing Cohen's blood to the DNA from the Shroud of Turin, but I destroyed the remnant of Cohen's blood," I say, more than regretful about the situation.

"What if that weren't the only sample?" he says, searching my face, as he motions for someone to enter the room. An officer walks into the room with a bloody white shirt.

It looks like the shirt Cohen was wearing when I last saw him. I gasp and immediately walk over to it as the officer steps back, acting as if he is almost afraid to hand it over to me. The officer is wearing gloves as he holds the shirt. He looks to Aki for permission to allow me to hold it. Aki nods. The officer allows me to accept it. I carefully bring it to my face, not touching the areas that have been saturated with blood. I bring it close enough to smell....It smells like baby detergent and outdoor air...It is undoubtedly Cohen's.

"It's Cohen's," I say, becoming tearful at the smell of it.

"It *is* Cohen's. You know how I know?" Aki says and, without waiting for my response, he continues, "I watched it fall from the sky. And it had this in the front pocket."

Aki offers me a folded piece of paper. I carefully place the shirt back in the dutiful hands of the other officer and accept the prayer from Aki.

"Something tells me you've seen it before," he says.

I open the note, a prayer, which reads, "God, if you exist, please show yourself to me." The handwriting is clearly mine and the authenticity is also confirmed by the typing on the back of the paper which reads, "You are accepted," revealing it was my prayer written on the acceptance letter from Johns Hopkins. I let the words of acceptance and the drastic display of miraculous love sink in. It's almost impossible for me to comprehend. I walk to my chair and sit to try to process everything.

"So this is what you will do...You will study the DNA from Cohen's shirt and compare it to that of the Shroud of Turin." I am so distracted by the love that I almost don't register Aki's statement. I have to use my short-term memory and repeat it to myself in my head and try to regain focus.

123

I give him a confused look and ask, "You have friends at the University of Texas?" This is where the Shroud of Turin is now kept under lock and key. Where, I have heard, DNA analysis has already been done on it and could only find genetic information for tooth enamel.

Aki restrains a smile. "I don't need friends at the University of Texas." He extends his hand to me, and I accept his help out of my chair. I walk with him as he ushers me out of the interrogation room, down the hall, past various Shin Bet officers who walk briskly by us, apparently on a mission. We enter the lobby area, near the door to the outside. Tré and Cameron are sitting on a leather couch. Tré rushes to my side.

"Are you okay?" he asks, giving me a hug and a kiss on my cheek.

"I'm fine."

"You are all free to leave. Thank you for your help." Aki shakes Tré's hand. Cameron shakes Aki's hand also and gives him a kiss on the cheek. He smiles warmly at her before he looks my way. "Journey, I will see you at Kfar Shaul Hospital at noon tomorrow," Aki says as he shakes my hand. I nod in agreement.

We walk outside, and a car is waiting to take us home. In the car, we all seem a little too nervous to say much. Tré's hand is caressing mine in a nurturing way.

"Well, I'm starving," Cameron says.

"So am I," I exclaim. I look at Tré.

"I could eat," he says.

"I'm buying," Cameron says with a smile. We remember she is now well endowed financially and congratulate her.

Cameron has the driver stop at the next restaurant, which is one of those odd-shaped buildings built to fit into a fork in the road. We waste no time ordering. The restaurant is swarming with people, and we talk about Cohen, totally engrossed in each other and the bond that we have. We recount our time with Cohen to each other, much as we did with Aki. Cameron tells us that the day the prayers fell was the first time that she had encountered Cohen. She says that the prayer that she handed to him was for an orphanage. She says that he tried to show her the face of God in the clouds on more than one occasion. She is ecstatic to learn that Tré was able to capture it on film. She warmheartedly laughs when she talks about the fear that we had of the Palestinian rockets. And she says that she loved carrying his secret and sharing the experience with him, of knowing what was veiled to us.

I love the fact that as much as I had valued my own intellect, I felt like I was the last to know about Cohen.

···

The next day I, Aki, and a rather impressive show of security escorts walk onto Dr. Oberstein's floor of Kfar Shaul Hospital. Dr. Oberstein, the nurse, and Yonathan look up, as Aki steps over to Dr. Oberstein.

"Dr. Oberstein. I want to thank you for all your support. Shin Bet would respectfully like to secure the use of your lab for official business. If you don't mind?" Aki asks politely.

Dr. Oberstein replies, "Please. Of course. Cooperating with security is my pleasure, and its priority has been communicated to all of my staff." His eyes shift slightly towards me as he continues, "I hope you find that this is true."

Aki pauses for the briefest moment, then says, "Yes. Thank you. Then, if you don't mind, Journey has agreed to work for us today."

Dr. Oberstein puts his arm around me. "Journey, it's good to see you. How are you?"

"Good," I say. "I am very happy to be helping them today," I say, assuring him.

Aki smiles.

"Please." Dr. Oberstein motions for Aki to continue onto the wing of the hospital. "I understand you have spoken to Melchizedek?" Dr. Oberstein gestures to Melchizedek in the dayroom. I see him there also.

"Yes." Aki confirms, not even looking toward Melchizedek, no longer interested but focused on the task at hand.

Dr. Oberstein looks over at me, "There is a blood sample here from Melchizedek. He's not an admit. He's clear. He has just agreed to participate in our research."

"If you don't mind, send his sample out…" I am only interested in studying the blood that we have with us.

I didn't even wonder then how confusing this all must have been for Dr. Oberstein, the man who is usually one step ahead of everything, including me.

I continue to walk to the lab with Aki, and the others with him. Once we are in the lab, Aki takes a case from one of the officers and opens it to present the Shroud remnant DNA that they had extracted.

"There's no reason these two *have* to be the same…" I say, suddenly worried about not coming up with the right results.

Aki looks at me. He looks impatient.

"I'm just saying…I just think that should be said," I assert. Now that I believe in God, I don't want anything, including forensic evidence, to take that away.

"Noted," says Aki, his impatience restrained for a brief moment. He gestures toward the sample.

I dare to pause momentarily to ask yet another question, "So the University of Texas just relinquished this to you?"

"What if *that* weren't the only sample?" he challenges me to widen the horizon of my thinking.

126

"Whose sample is this?" I ask.

"It now belongs to Mossad.

"Mossad?" I ask. FBI is to Shin Bet as CIA is to Mossad. I only now realize I missed that question on the standardized test for grad school, and I'm ticked. Focus.

"You would be surprised how much security and religion are intertwined...This is Israel." He smiles, amusing himself with my reaction. After all of this, I have no idea of what kind of look I must be giving him.

With the sample securely in place, I take a look into my testing equipment. I don't know what I was expecting... but I was looking at normal human DNA. Not something that could cure the diseases of the day or replace stem cells, or in any way suggest immortality. I carefully return the sample to its protective case.

"A lot more than tooth enamel, but something tells me you already know that," I say. I take a deep breath in as I am handed the DNA extracted from Cohen's shirt.

I take a look. My brain doesn't quite register what I start to see before all I can see is brown carpet... I try to take a breath because I know what's coming... and yellow flowers...It's too late. Yellow pulsating flowers and the muted brown give way to Aki's face. I realize that I am in his arms. I still have the pins and needles sensation in my nose, as I pull on his arms to stand.

"Are you okay?" he asks.

"I'm fine. I'm more than fine...I'm in awe. The DNA is the same. It's exactly the same."

Aki helps me up and I can't help it. I start jumping up and down. I hug Aki, and he, surprisingly, gives a warm enthusiastic hug back.

...

127

When everything is back in its place, Aki escorts me out of the lab. As we walk by, I see that Melchizedek is still in the dayroom. I turn to Dr. Oberstein, who is seated at the nurse's station.

"I thought you said he wasn't admitted?" I ask him.

"He's waiting to talk to you," Dr. Oberstein explains.

Aki shakes Dr. Oberstein's hand. "Dr. Oberstein, thank you for your hospitality," he says.

"It was my pleasure," Dr. Oberstein replies.

Aki turns toward me and gives me a warm handshake, taking my hand in both of his. "I will see you when you finish documenting your findings," Aki says. It is an order. It is an invitation. It is totally Aki.

"Yes, thank you," I reply.

"Call me." He smiles and winks at me. I smile back, assuming he is referring to the ordeal that my last phone call was for him. I walk into the dayroom to meet Melchizedek.

Melchizedek gestures toward himself, introducing himself correctly for the first time, "Scott," he says. Hereafter, I will refer to him, not as Melchizedek, but Scott.

"Thank you for waiting for me," I say.

We talk about our experience together. It is really nice to get to know more about him. He tells me that he is a seminary student from Pasadena, California. In contrast to his Melchizedek persona, he actually seems a little shy.

As we exit the dayroom together, Scott gives me a heartfelt hug goodbye. I turn to find Dr. Oberstein waiting.

"You're still here?" I ask.

"*I* was waiting to talk to you. I wanted to let you know…you still have as much time as you need…to return to your work here," he says.

"Are you trying to get rid of me?" I ask jokingly. "Did you hire someone else?"

128

He puts his arm around me as he walks me out. "You will *always* have a position here, regardless of the grant. And I anxiously await your return," he assures me.

Chapter Ten

That same night, Tré and I hold hands as we walk to our first Israeli partner dancing lesson. It's dusk, and there are just a few people out in the city.

"I'm really proud of you," he says.

"It was really exciting today. The fact that the Shroud and Cohen's blood are identical proves the miraculous...The odds of that happening by chance are astronomical. I am excited, but I'm not sure if it will confuse people that the DNA, as far as I could tell, was simple human DNA," I say.

"It never occurred to me that it wouldn't be normal DNA. He clothed himself in *humanity*."

"I am a little afraid that the research might be misunderstood, or that it will only be understood by geneticists or theologians," I confess.

"With God, there has always been a veil of mystery...it's a given that some people won't understand it. All you can do is move when He moves. It's just like when you sparred with Cohen or when you danced with him. When He moves...you move. In Psalms it says, 'He guides us with His eye.' He has led you to this research, exquisitely, from the time you viewed the Shroud, as a child...to discussing the replica of it at my apartment. This is the direction he has led you in. You are doing what you are supposed to do. Just leave the results up to Him."

"Thank you," I say, and I try to breathe in his words like the truth I believe they are. At that, he gives me a quick kiss.

We climb the steps to the building where our dance class is held. We sign in and pay the small fee for the dance session.

The music starts and people begin to dance to warm up. We join them, and I let Tré's words ring true as he leads me on the dance floor.

...

A couple of days later, back at my apartment, I sit at my laptop. I stop typing, and then look at the screen sideways.

I finished typing my report, and although I thought what it communicated was of course utterly amazing, I felt boxed in when I wrote it, as if the report wasn't enough…if that's possible.

I begin to print the document. I search through my purse and find Aki's card. I dial his number, and as I hear his line starting to ring…there is a knock at the door.

Aki answers my call, "Hello, Journey, would you mind opening the door?" I open the door to Aki, who presses the END CALL button.

I smile as I say, "You have some remarkable timing." I open the door even wider, and he walks in.

"Well, you're not bad yourself," he says.

"Seriously, I was just printing out the report." I take the papers out of the printer and try to hand them to him. He looks at the papers, as if the gesture was pointless.

"I've already read it," he confesses.

"How…?" I start to question him, but then I look at the computer and then back at him. "You're good…What did you think?"

"It's thorough, well written, and ready for public announcement," he says. I start to let out the breath I have been holding in, only to stop short as he speaks again.

He circles me, as he walks. "It doesn't quite seem to capture *everything* that should be told."

"Well said," I agree.

"I have a confession for you. I envy you, and Cameron, and Tré. For obvious reasons...your time with Cohen...but also because I am a man with a story I cannot tell...I can't publicize my healing. My obscurity is my defense...and this of course is the nature of my work." He admits his frustration.

"Are you suggesting that I write about our experiences with Cohen for Shin Bet?"

"No...not for *Shin Bet*."

"I will do it," I reply without hesitation.

"Good...then we will spar another day," he says as if he is not above coercion. With a smile and a wink, he walks out.

It was only moments after he left that I returned to my laptop and began to write. Within the guidelines that would please Aki...I wrote every secret, I wrote every lie...I wrote to understand...I wrote to be understood....and I wrote about the *feeling*...but I think Cameron may have said it better...There's no translation.

I spent most days and evenings engrossed in writing. But I was committed to telling the story properly. And there were interesting events still occurring that made the writing even better.

•••

Tré and I walk over to Cohen's apartment, Michal's house, to admire his work. We kneel down, and I point to the first stone that he had laid, the one that I had at first rejected. "This is the one," I say.

132

Just then, Michal opens the door of her house and walks out to join us.

"I never get tired of looking at it either." She joins our conversation, familiar with the context.

"I wish we could date it. I would like to think he created this with the appearance of age," I say, half-quoting Cohen.

"You know my friends are archeologists," Michal says. "We can."

"But carbon-14 dating is for organic matter...," I say, arguing that it can't be done.

"They are now able to test the mortar. I will have it done."

...

Later that evening, Tré and I are once again kissing at the doorway. Things with Tré are still wonderfully complicated...We break away from each other, and he hands me my keys and turns and walks away, as I close the door.

The next day we are in my apartment sparring. So even though things are just as complicated, we have developed ways of working them out.

...

I go with Cameron to view Cohen's hotel. My realtor is showing it, and she walks us through the hotel. We marvel at the work of his hands; the grandeur of the marble pillars, the high ceilings adorned with shimmering chandeliers and crown molding. It vaguely reminds me of modern-day overpriced, upscale chain restaurants; only everything was real. You couldn't tap the hollow in these marble pillars, and believe me...I tried.

The realtor begins her sales pitch to Cameron, "You know the economy has changed so much since the discovery of oil—congratulations, dear—that the original buyers defaulted. It was a partnership between an Israeli and a foreign investor. Are you interested in buying the hotel?" the realtor asks.

"I just came to see it. I thought Journey had communicated that to you," Cameron says in curt Israeli style.

"She did, and I am more than happy to show it to you," the realtor says with American Southern charm. The realtor weaves us in and out of the hotel rooms and suites, but pauses in front of a particular door as she puts the key card in it. "Now I have just showed you a room that is a typical suite for the hotel. This room that I'm about to show you is just kind of a conversation piece. One of the workers on the building painted this room, and it was not part of the original design," she says. The realtor opens the door to a pink and purple room complete with butterflies and flower decor.

"Yes, it was," Cameron says, meaning that it was part of the original design. "I'll take it," she says, with the pink and purple reflected in her huge pupils.

...

As I am entering the pathway to my yard, Michal comes out of the door to her house. "Journey, you were right," she says. "The mortar dates back a thousand years, consistent with the original architectural remains," Michal says excitedly.

"Oh, Michal, thank you for sharing that. This is very exciting, and it helps my work," I say. The restoration, when it was created, had an appearance of age.

Just then, I realize that a car has pulled up and is waiting with the window down. I see that Dr. Oberstein is at the wheel.

"Journey," he calls.

I walk up to his car. "Hi, it's good to see you. Would you like to come in?"

"No, thank you. I have to get home. Have you enjoyed your time off?" he asks.

"Yes," I reply.

He gets right to the point. "Are you coming back?"

"I will come in and talk to you tomorrow," I say.

"You're not coming back?" he deduces.

"No," I reply. "Thank you for everything."

"I understand and wish you the best," he says. He puts his hand to the wheel. And at that, I turn to walk away.

"Journey?" I hear him call to me.

"Yes," I say, turning around.

"You'll keep in touch?" he asks.

"Of course," I say.

...

Tré's mother, Pat, comes to visit, and I cook a meal of salmon, sautéed vegetables, and rice. She is a pleasant woman, and you can almost tell by her clear skin and smile lines that she is a woman who smiles often and has lived well.

"Thank you, Journey. That meal was great," she says genuinely. She looks over at Tré. "Tré, you didn't tell me she could cook, too."

"Well, we go out a lot, Mom," he says honestly, because we try to not be alone too often.

I get up to take Tré's and his mother's empty dishes to the sink. Pat takes my face in her hands. "You're his solace," she says adoringly.

Tré leans forward and looks at her ring closely. "Mom, did you know you are missing a diamond from your engagement ring?" She still wore it. Pat examines her hand. She takes off her ring and looks at it. Fortunately, the main, princess-cut diamond is securely in place. One of the smaller diamonds in the setting is missing from the antique band of the ring.

"Oh, no. I didn't need this…not now," she says sadly. Tré takes the ring from her, and slips it in his pocket to take it off of her mind.

"If we don't find it, I will have it replaced. This is Israel; they have the best cuts of diamonds in the world," he assures her.

"Thank you, darling. I plan to wear it until you're ready to give it to someone," she says suggestively, as she looks my way and smiles.

It's not long before Pat leaves to go to the hotel to "rest" her legs. Tré and I go out onto the balcony and into the golden sunlight of the early evening. The view is captivating, as always, but we still can't help but look at each other.

"I love you *so* much," Tré says. His eyes are beaming, and he looks excited, almost nervous.

"I love you, too," I respond with a little kiss and hug. I realize that this is the first time these words have been said, and it surprises me that we didn't speak them before. The words went unnoticeably absent because the feeling always seemed so very apparent. Tré looks out at the horizon as if he is searching for something. Then he looks back at me.

"Cohen and I talked about you," he says with a smile, luring me eagerly into this conversation.

"What did he say?" I ask with undivided attention.

"He said that I was afraid to commit."

"And are you?"

"I was…He said I could be standing with the perfect woman, under a rainbow, with a ring in my pocket…and I would be afraid to commit. Only I can't find a rainbow, and I don't feel afraid." Tré gets down on one knee. He takes my hand in his and continues, "I don't want to give you a broken ring…but you took me when I was broken." He reaches in his pocket. "Journey, will you marry me?" He presents the ring

136

to me. He slides the ring on my finger. I pull his sweet face to mine, as he stands. We kiss. My soul is relieved by his promise of a future.

"I didn't hear you say yes…did you say yes?" he asks with his boyish smile.

"Yes!" I say enthusiastically.

"Yeah, you just went right for that ring," he jokes.

We both look at the ring, thinking about the promise it symbolizes. We look out onto the city, hopeful about our future.

…

The next night, Tré and I celebrate our engagement in an Armenian restaurant in the Old City. The waitress brings out three glasses of wine, which for a moment confuses us. We look over as Aki surprises us with a visit and sits down with us.

"I understand congratulations are in order," Aki says knowingly.

"Nothing gets by you," I say, impressed.

"Mazel tov," he says raising his glass to us. Tré and I toast with him and smile at each other. Before we put our glasses down, Aki adds, "Journey, your writing is going well."

"Thank you," I say, knowing that he has read it, through his own resources.

"When will it be finished?" he asks eagerly.

"After the wedding," I reply.

"I take it this will be soon?" Aki says, almost demandingly.

"What are you doing next week?" I say, glad to accommodate.

"You don't mess around," he says, impressed.

"We've waited long enough," Tré replies.

Aki nods understandingly and then looks at me adoringly. "Journey, Dr. Oberstein informed me that you have quit your job."

"Yes," I say, never surprised by his research.

"You believe your writing is *that* good?" he asks.

"You tell me," I say challengingly.

"I will be the first to admit—you are good at what you do," he says. He changes the subject, "I understand that you are looking into making Aliyah." Not the least bit questioning.

"I am," I say. I had done an Internet search into the matter.

"Immigration can be a tough road," he says. "A lot of paperwork and details."

"A geneticist, with a name like Kaufmann...I think I have more than a fighting chance," I say, half-offended.

Aki reaches into his pocket and takes out two passports, handing one to me and one to Tré. We open them and discover that we have dual citizenship in Israel and the United States. We stare at them like they are gold. I reach over and hug Aki and kiss his cheek. He looks a little embarrassed and looks towards Tré, who shakes his hand and enthusiastically thanks him.

Aki says, "You shouldn't be worried with those details. You have a wedding to plan and a book to finish. You are good at what you do: We allow you certain privileges. Consider it a wedding gift. I should go, I'm working. I just dropped by to say 'Mazel tov.'" He downs the rest of his wine and gestures with the glass. "They allow me certain privileges." He looks over at me and says, "Journey, we will spar another day." He pats Tré on the back and winks. He stands up, pretends to check if his gun is still there, flashes a warm smile and then walks out.

138

...

We liked the Armenian restaurant so much that we have decided to have our rehearsal dinner there. It's not a large wedding party, so it wasn't too difficult to book. My sister, Cindy, and Tré hit it off right away. I didn't really get why they started calling each other "Maverick" and "Iceman," but they seemed to enjoy it, so I didn't mind. My mother, who never drinks and thinks it's a sin, ended up drinking champagne because her "throat" was "tight." I have never seen her so happy. She offered everyone she met a glass. Tré's mother was as polite and assuring as ever. We gave her an early birthday present, a Roman glass ring from an Israeli designer.

Chapter Eleven

We choose to get married in the garden of Gethsemane, in the late afternoon. I am wearing a strapless A-line wedding dress covered in "old lace" to include an all-lace train. My hair is pulled up and secured with a circular pearl headpiece that has the veil hanging from it down my back. A few loose curls fall stray along my neck.

"Journey, you look…stunning," Aki says, as he offers his arm to walk me down the aisle.

"Thank you," I say, as I slide my arm into his. Standing this close to him, I can feel that he is wearing his gun. "You wore your gun to my wedding?" I whisper as we start to walk down the aisle.

"I sleep with it," he replies.

I smile at his remark. Then I am truly taken back by the sight of everyone turning to stand as we walk down the aisle together. My heart is overwhelmed at seeing the faces of family and friends in the place that I love. It feels a bit surreal, but also warm and fully ordained by God. I walk toward Tré, who looks impeccable in his classic tux with a white necktie. I walk slowly toward him completely encompassed in the present and yet eager to reach him. He smiles as I reach him and gestures for me to look up. I look up to see a beautiful rainbow in the sky, not a storm cloud in sight.

Tré and I stand face to face as Scott sings beautifully. Tré's minister then leads us as we exchange our sacred vows to love each other; "to have and to hold from this day forward, for better or for worse, for richer, for poorer, in sickness and in health, to love and to cherish; from this day forward till death do us part." Tré is then asked to place the wedding band on my hand. He slips it on. Our eyes, which have been locked lovingly on each other, look down at the rings. We stare at the perfect and complete circle of stones in his mother's engagement ring, my ring. Oddly enough, in the circle of white diamonds, shines one chocolate diamond.

"Did you do that?" Tré whispers.

I smile at him, then marvel at the stone, "The ring hasn't left my hand since you put it on."

"That's so Cohen. It's like your one brown eye," he whispers.

He restores brokenness.

I am asked to place the ring on Tré's finger and do. We are pronounced man and wife.

This moment is powerfully surreal, as Tré's pupils dance with the flash from the pictures that are being taken.

This is the moment that I dreamed of as a child, later wondering whether it would ever really happen. And it did. I thought standing there that it might actually be the moment for our Lord to return, as if there was something penultimate about it.

...

Our reception is held in the hotel that Cohen built. Yes, it was an orphanage, but Cameron manages to use it for many things: church, weddings, whatever she felt the Lord was in.

Tré and I are entangled in an intimate Israeli partner dance. As entranced as I am with him, I can't help finding myself looking for Cohen. I can't escape the thought that at any moment I might see His face again as Tré and I dance in the room that was built by His hands.

He was preparing a place for us, and He would come again…but it was not that day.

…

We stayed there at the hotel that night. I loved that Tré held to the tradition of carrying me over the threshold into our room. We shared a moment on the balcony praying and thanking the Lord for our marriage and our beautiful wedding, telling Him that we anxiously await the marriage feast in heaven. We feel thankful to have such a beautiful analogy to it, through our own day.

Then we commenced with the consecration of our marriage with all the love and passion that we have always had. No, with unequivocally more.

…

The next morning, the light shines through the window. Tré is half-lying on me as we sleep. His unbridled hands start moving with intent on my body, with no regret, before he even opens his eyes.

We spent our honeymoon at several resorts in Israel, because really there is no place that we'd rather be. The honeymoon flew by and was a much-needed therapeutic rest. I was refreshed and inspired enough to finish my writing when we returned. And I did finish it.

…

A few months later, I find myself back at Cohen's hotel. A woman walks down the hallway, past impressive framed photos, the last one being that of Cohen, Cameron, and the face in the clouds. There Cohen's shirt is also on display, always with an armed Israeli officer nearby, as Aki had arranged. The book is a huge success. I hold signings in the hall there, where I can watch people view Tré's photographs, which are equally successful. Whenever I'm signing, I always stop when I see a little girl standing before Cohen's shirt; it reminds me of myself, as a child.

I finish signing the book that is in my hands. My ring sparkles in the light.

Oh, and about the diamond. We were told that its clarity exactly matched that of the others in the ring, not without imperfection...the cut was flawless.

As I am signing, I am handed another book and a picture.

I was often handed pictures by tourists who were "just wondering" if they had encountered Cohen. Sometimes it would be pictures of Scott; most of the time it would be someone I had never seen; it was never Cohen. Tré too, was handed pictures of sightings in the clouds and he graciously said that he could see them all.

I finish signing the book and regretfully tell the lady that her picture is not of Cohen. She exits, and I see that Elizabeth stands before me. I stand up and go over to hug her.

"I was late that day. I wish I could have been there," she says about the day that Cohen and Scott spoke, the day Cohen walked over the hill and disappeared.

"Me, too," I say empathetically.

She begins, "I was looking through my pictures after I read your book because I remembered a girl who fainted when I went to see the Shroud of Turin nineteen years ago." She takes the picture out of the book I wrote and hands it to me. "And I was just wondering..." I look at the picture and see...a muted brown. Familiar yellow flowers emerge....and give way to a picture of Cohen holding me when I was a child. He is looking right into the camera. His eyes are knowing; his smile soft. The exposure on his wrists and hands looks a little blown out.

•••

I stand with Tré in the darkroom where he processes his photographs. Elizabeth was actually able to find the negative from the picture of me and Cohen. Tré is manually developing the picture from the negative. I stand nervously and excitedly at his side, afraid to touch anything except, of course, him.

Tré exposes the image to light and "burns" the image of Cohen and me onto the photographic paper. Then he uses a piece of cardboard with a hole in the middle (a photographic developing, burning technique) to expose only Cohen's hands to the light for a little longer. When he is satisfied, he places the picture in the developer bath. When the picture slowly appears, Cohen's wrists are properly exposed, revealing healed circular wound scars.

I am speechless at the poetic way that Cohen has continued to reveal himself to me. I thought it odd after writing that I still chose to use the name, Cohen, which I began to know Him as. It might seem more appropriate to some to call Him...

THE END

ACKNOWLEDGEMENTS

I would like to thank the Lord, My God, through whom all blessings flow. I truly believe that this is our work – something we did together, because so much of this book was just too easy for *me* to write. I think it portrays your depth, mystery, and allure. All the things I love about you.

I am very thankful for my husband, Mark, who is the hardest worker that I know. It is a joy to have you as my partner in life. Every day you are the living example of the love of God. I love you with my whole heart and words just don't seem to capture how grateful I am for you. Thank you for all the times you made time for me to write and for inspiring me to continue.

Thank you to my children, who have said many prayers for this book to succeed. I am counting on them. Both of you inspire me to live a purpose driven life and I pray that your lives will be purpose driven. Thank you for teaching me through your prayers, as you are committed to praying for "God's people," firemen, soldiers, policemen, and "people who help us." You are truly about the work of God.

Thank you to my mother, Jackie Bodden, for setting an example in so many things. You are an awesome writer and have given me inspiration to believe that I can do this.

Thank you to my dad, who didn't quite understand why I went to Israel when I did. I have a feeling you do now. I miss you.

Thank you to my beautiful niece Madelyn, for giving Journey a face and this book a stunning cover. I think the picture captures everything Journey is…intrigued, in love, determined…spiritual. Thank you for not hesitating to share the beauty God has given you. Thank you for having James Dylan as a friend and awesome photographer, who was equally as gracious to offer help. You both are true artists.

I am so thankful to all my family and friends who have offered love and support. You give a dreamer courage!

Thank you to my husband's awesome friends, Randy Field, Ben Hornby, and Daniel Reany. Randy worked tirelessly in collaboration with Mark to sculpt this beautiful cover. Ben Hornby proofed my work and offered a keen editing eye. Daniel Reany was my published author "mentor." I thank you and Ben for letting me know that the major plot point worked.

I am also thankful to Jamie Stewart for welcoming me into her home in Israel and for being a thoughtful tour guide. Had I not went to Israel, this book would never have been.

I have to thank Gideon Weiss, who I heard speak when I thought that my book was finished. Needless to say, a certain scene that had already been written was lacking the "fireworks" that it now has.

Thank you to Aki, who agreed to read a screenplay I hadn't quite written. I wrote feverishly in those two weeks with the thought of you reading it. The character of Aki evolved greatly because of your interest.

Thank you to the reader. This story is for you and inspired by you. I hope you enjoy it. Thank you to those of you who are willing to take the time to write a review or share your thoughts on social media. The success of this book is largely in your hands.